Miss Windermere Woos a Highlander

Windermeres in Love Series
Book Three

Sofie Darling

Dragonblade Publishing, Inc. is an imprint of Kathryn Le Veque Novels, Inc.
P.O. Box 23
Moreno Valley, CA 92556
ceo@dragonbladepublishing.com

Produced in the United States of America

First Edition November 2022
Trade Paperback Edition

ARE YOU SIGNED UP FOR DRAGONBLADE'S BLOG?

You'll get the latest news and information on exclusive giveaways, exclusive excerpts, coming releases, sales, free books, cover reveals and more.

Check out our complete list of authors, too!

No spam, no junk. That's a promise!

Sign Up Here

www.dragonbladepublishing.com

Dearest Reader;

Thank you for your support of a small press. At Dragonblade Publishing, we strive to bring you the highest quality Historical Romance from some of the best authors in the business. Without your support, there is no 'us', so we sincerely hope you adore these stories and find some new favorite authors along the way.

Happy Reading!

CEO, Dragonblade Publishing

Additional Dragonblade books by Author Sofie Darling

Windermeres in Love Series
Mr. Sinclair Beguiles a Bluestocking (Prequel)
Lady Amelia Takes a Lover (Book 1)
Lord Archer Catches a Contessa (Book 2)
Miss Windermere Woos a Highlander (Book 3)

Prologue

Italian countryside
March 1820

IT HAD BEEN a perfect day—the Tuscan sun warm and inviting, tall grasses swaying in the gentle country breeze—the day Miss Juliet Windermere decided Lord Rory Macbeth, Viscount Kilmuir and future Sixth Earl of Carrick, could take a flying leap off a Scottish mountain.

Ben Nevis would do.

She'd been rambling through a small grove of olive trees, taking in the bright Italian air—the feel of it in her lungs, against the bare skin of her arms—the members of their party thrown to the four winds. Amelia painting by a stream. Delilah reciting lines from Marlowe in a field. Archie and his friends charming a passel of opera singers brought over from Florence with their *joie de vivre* and prosecco.

For her part, Juliet had wandered off—as she was wont to do when the mood struck—to be alone with her own words for a while. Her cousins loved to talk, and she loved to listen and let the words swirl around her mind before committing them to paper. She'd even had a necklace specially made with a large locket containing bits of paper that she wore everywhere. No word—or configuration thereof—would ever be lost.

Then it happened.

In the not-too-far distance, she caught a tree in the periphery of her vision. Not a tree of gnarled twists and turns like the eternal olive, but one thick and solid like an oak one would find in England.

The tree moved.

The tree, it turned out, wasn't a tree at all, but a man. A rather large hulking man with light red hair that shone the gold of an autumn sunset; bright, opaque blue eyes the hue of a turquoise stone; and an ever-present lopsided smile.

A Scotsman, in fact.

And not just any Scotsman, but the Scotsman with whom she'd been besotted from the time Archie had brought him home from Eton during a school holiday and introduced him as Rory.

And now, she was alone with him.

She caught the instant he noticed her, and the lopsided smile found its way to his mouth. He gave a small wave of greeting, which she returned like for like.

No more, no less.

That was the key to keeping an infatuation secret. *Like for like… No more, no less.*

No one ever had to know if she never gave herself away.

"A fellow wanderer," he said, making light conversation in his rumbly Scottish burr that had been known to set butterflies aflight in her stomach.

Her mouth lifted into a smile of greeting—*no more, no less.* "Ah, yes."

He drifted toward her, absently snapping a tiny branch off an olive tree. Juliet did the same. Once they'd come within ten or so feet of each other—comfortable talking distance—he stopped, and she stopped. It was close enough that she caught his scent. Clean, as always, with an earthy hint of pine. How was it that he smelled of Scottish pine forests here in Italy?

Sometimes she wondered if she was infatuated with the man himself, or with the idea of him… Then she looked at him and knew it was the man himself. He was so burly and strong and handsome. It was true. But he was also so very nice. An appealing combination in a man, it had to be acknowledged.

His brow crinkled, and his head cocked to the side. He was staring…at *her*…as if he was only now seeing her for the first time, so centered she felt within his gaze—a place in which she'd never before found herself.

Those butterflies in her stomach multiplied, fluttering through her chest, and making it difficult to breathe.

He closed the distance between them in a few easy strides, and she found herself frozen in place, unable to do naught but wait for his next movement. He reached out and pushed an escaped tendril of hair off her face, and a realization struck her.

This was the moment in the farthest, most secret corner of her heart she'd been waiting for since he'd joined their party in Florence several days ago.

His hand moved down her face…and plucked a dandelion seed off her cheek. He held it up and opened forefinger and thumb, releasing it to the wind.

She emitted a nervous, little laugh that didn't sound like her in the least. Miss Juliet Windermere was known for her calm nature and quick wit. She was no vapid miss who giggled at the fiddle-faddle of gentlemen. But now, with the object of her secret infatuation standing so near and staring down at her looking serious and intent and so very, very handsome, she hadn't the faintest notion how to be.

"I've never noticed something about you," he rumbled.

Juliet's butterflies gave her heart wing. Her palms slicked with perspiration. "Oh?" she asked, breathless.

"You exactly resemble—"

A raven-haired Botticelli? Venus di Milo, but with arms and a head?

"Who?" she breathed.

"Miss Davina Dalhousie."

Juliet blinked, and whatever dreamy expression she'd been directing at him froze on her face.

Miss Davina Dalhousie.

Of course.

The lady who had rejected his proposal of marriage before he'd hied off to Italy. Yet…

For a moment, the possibility had existed that his infatuation for Miss Dalhousie had faded—apparently, the young lady had been quite definite in her rejection—and Juliet herself had, at last, caught his eye.

But, alas, that wasn't the reality.

In an instant, she knew what she needed to do. First, get as far away from this man as quickly as possible. Second, have a good, cleansing cry. And, lastly and most importantly, write a verse where the villain of the piece tragically slips and falls off a Scottish mountain or is rammed in the bum by a het up Highland coo.

The latter scenario held a particular appeal as the butterflies in her stomach were replaced by bats—the sort that gnawed.

"Like Miss Dalhousie?" she said around the unresolved sob in her throat. Somehow, her voice sounded remarkably like hers— cool and composed.

In other words, she sounded remarkably—*blessedly*—like herself.

"Her hair is dark, like yours," he said, apparently oblivious to the murderous narrowing of Juliet's eyes.

"The resemblance sounds uncanny."

His eyebrows gathered. He might've caught the note of sarcasm. "Have I said something to offend you?"

"Of course not." She pressed a palm to her forehead. "My head has begun to ache, and I would like a lie down."

It wasn't a complete fib. She would like to lie down.

He nodded and let it pass.

Amongst the whirl of other emotions, Juliet experienced relief. She simply wanted to ask where he was going and leg it in the opposite direction.

She offered a mumble of farewell and fled, determination pushing through embarrassment and irritation and settling solid and deep inside her gut.

She would leave this secret infatuation with the Viscount Kilmuir here, in this Italian olive grove, and never again give it light to grow.

She'd been an utter fool.

Never again.

Chapter One

Scottish Highlands
April 1822

RORY RUSHED INTO the receiving hall of Dalhousie Manor and tried not to feel like the conspicuously ill-mannered guest that he was.

The hall, a grand, square room surrounded on all four sides by three levels of open corridors with a large skylight above, was blessedly empty.

He flicked a clod of muck off the sleeve of his greatcoat.

The fact was he was late.

A problem had arisen at Baile Ìm that was beyond his control and had demanded as speedy a resolution as possible.

Namely, a roiling case of frothy bloat.

Not in him, of course, but his sheep.

Unable to resist a field of spring barley, a group of a dozen sheep had snuck in and feasted on the delicacy to their heart's content—but not that of their stomachs. So, it had been a treatment of mineral oil to get them all sorted, which had taken painstaking time.

Which had made him late for his neighbor's supper party.

He flicked more mud off his sleeve. He'd already been dressed for the evening when the frothy bloat emergency had come to light, and he hadn't time to change clothes before rushing here.

His father—the Earl of Carrick—had gifted him Baile Ìm after his return from Italy, as a way of preparing him for his future duties. "No son of mine will be throwing all I built into ruin."

Da's exact words.

And fair enough.

Rory had arrived a year ago determined to prove himself capable of succeeding at the honor and responsibility Da had bestowed upon him. He liked the work. Further, he liked that Baile Ìm neighbored Dalhousie Manor—which included supper party invitations. A boon for a bachelor laird, truth told.

Tonight's gathering was to introduce their newly-arrived guests to the area. Of course, Rory was already well acquainted with Lady Delilah and Miss Juliet Windermere. Delilah was sister to his closest friend, Viscount Archer—known to all as Archie—and Miss Windermere was their cousin who had lived with them since she was in leading strings—a sister for all intents and purposes. Didn't say much, Miss Windermere.

Of course, who could get a word in edgewise in a house full of Windermeres.

He'd just handed his greatcoat to Rivers, Dalhousie Manor's ancient butler, when a figure appeared at the far end of the hall. Rory's body lit with recognition. "Miss Dalhousie," he called out before thinking better of the familiarity.

It was improper, of course, but he couldn't help himself. When he'd first arrived to take possession of Baile Ìm, he'd thought his proximity might lead Miss Dalhousie to reconsider his marriage proposal, but very quickly he'd seen his nearness had no effect.

It had been surprisingly easy to shrug off the whole misbegotten idea.

Now, he noted a stiffness to her shoulders and an uncharacteristic rapidity to her step. Miss Dalhousie never held herself or moved so.

His head cocked. The woman approaching him was…

Tall.

Like a…

Windermere.

Raven-black hair parted in the center and pulled back into a chignon at the base of her neck and dressed in a moss-green silk evening gown that heightened the clear emerald hue of her eyes, it wasn't Miss Davina Dalhousie approaching.

But Miss Juliet Windermere.

Rory's mouth stretched into an instinctive smile of recognition, and his hand lifted in a small wave of greeting.

She returned neither. Her eyes only narrowed on him.

Though he'd known Miss Windermere for over a decade, he'd never held the impression that she much cared for him. For starters, she was always scowling at him.

Like now.

Further, if the rapid clip of her heels didn't let up, she would barrel directly into him. He was bracing himself for impact when she came to a dead stop three feet away.

At nearly six feet and four inches, he was accustomed to standing head and shoulders above every woman he met. Not so with Miss Windermere. She stood only an inch or two below six feet, her gaze nearly meeting his on an equal plane.

"Miss Windermere," he said, at a loss for any other words.

Something new struck him. He'd always thought her very similar to Miss Dalhousie, but actually the two women bore little resemblance to one another, other than a similar hair color. Where Miss Dalhousie's eyes were a lovely, limpid brown, Miss Windermere's were the sort of jewel green that could cut, if one wasn't careful. Where Miss Dalhousie's face was a smooth oval, Miss Windermere's was the exact shape of a heart. Miss Dalhousie's nose was a cute, little button; Miss Windermere's long and aquiline.

Miss Dalhousie was pretty as a picture.

And Miss Windermere was…

Absolutely, devastatingly beautiful.

How had he never noticed that about her?

Without a return of his greeting, she reached up. For a wild instant, he thought she might slide her silk-gloved hand around his neck and pull his head down for a kiss.

And for an equally wild instant, he thought he might not mind too much.

Instead, she struck forefinger against thumb and flicked his right cheekbone.

A gob of dried mud flew across the room.

A befuddled beat of silence followed before he recovered and said, "Erm, thank you."

She nodded curtly and brushed past, continuing on her way as if he'd been naught more than a minor inconvenience, her skirts an efficient silk swish in her wake.

His eye lingered an instant longer than necessary on that efficient swish of her skirts.

He gave himself a mental shake. Miss Windermere was practically a sister to his closest friend in the world.

Right.

Slowly, he followed her, for presumably she was making her way toward the dining room. Her legs were long enough that when she got them moving at a rapid clip, she could cover a great deal of ground in a hurry.

If he didn't know better, he'd think she was attempting to place as much distance between herself and him as quickly as possible as they traversed one corridor after another. Though he was going to supper, it occurred to him that, really, he might be following Miss Windermere.

Strange, that.

Truly, though, what had just happened?

The facts were that he'd had a gob of mud on his face and Miss Windermere had done him the great favor of disposing of it. Except…

It didn't feel like a favor.

It felt like an act of aggression.

Which left but one question.

What had he ever done to invite Miss Juliet Windermere's wrath?

He stepped into the dining room and found a lively gathering already in progress. Servants rushing to and fro, filling wine glasses, readying the first course at the buffet. Mr. and Mrs. Dalhousie were seated at opposite ends of the table with all their guests and family between them—neighbors Mr. and Mrs. Robertson; guests of honor Delilah and Miss Windermere—who was presently being guided to her seat—a few more neighbors; the condescending Mr. Oliver Quincy who seemed to have a relative in every corner of England, Scotland, and Wales; and all the young Dalhousie offspring scattered throughout, including Miss Dalhousie. Rory was relieved to find her seated down the table from the chair he was being ushered toward.

Relief was short-lived, however. For as he was lowering into his seat, he found himself directly across from Miss Windermere, who was studiously considering the tines of her fish fork.

She'd noticed, too.

His host's voice rang out from the head of the table. "If it isn't Kilmuir," said Mr. Dalhousie, checking his pocket watch for all to see. "And nearly on time, too," he finished with a hearty, unoffended laugh.

"The sheep," began Kilmuir, the tips of his ears burning, as they always did when he felt in the wrong.

"Ah, my boy, this is Scotland," said his host. "It's always the sheep."

This provoked a good round of chuckles around the table.

Rory felt another sort of heat on the side of his face—the heat of a stare. His gaze shifted, and he found Miss Windermere's emerald eyes upon him. Reflexively, his mouth curved into a smile. Her gaze widened for an instant before startling away.

He followed her line of sight to find Delilah at the other end. *Of course.* Those two had been close all their lives—since Miss Windermere had come to live with her uncle, aunt, and cousins after her parents perished in a tragic carriage accident. With

Delilah being the more conversable of the two, Rory hadn't taken much notice of Miss Windermere beyond the fact that she was a relation of Archie's and pleasant to be around in the general sense.

Until ten minutes ago.

Of a sudden, he intuited a truth about Miss Windermere. Unlike her cousin, she preferred to blend into the background. So, she used Delilah as a shield. He'd never really noticed her because she didn't wish to be noticed.

Which was quite the trick, considering how striking she was. Those blush-pink lips. Those high, delicate cheekbones. Those emerald eyes that could peer into a soul and tell its secrets...eyes that contained both an openness and a mystery.

What had happened this last year that Miss Windermere had transformed into a siren?

"Lady Delilah," said their hostess from her end of the table, "what news do you bring of your family?"

Delilah finished her sip of wine. "If Mama and Papa's ship didn't encounter any trouble on the Mediterranean, I believe they should be in Greece by now."

"Greece?" asked Mrs. Robertson in her soft Scottish burr, a horrified expression on her face.

"Mount Pelion, to be precise," continued Delilah, her crystalline blue eyes sparkling with mischief, delighting in horrifying upright ladies.

Where Miss Windermere was a dark-haired beauty, Delilah's blonde curls cropped above her shoulders provided a light contrast. Apparently, short hair on a woman was considered scandalous, but Rory couldn't see why. The style suited Delilah's fine-boned features perfectly.

He gave a mental shrug. Ladies tended to construct such arbitrary rules for themselves. He supposed they got bored.

"Isn't that correct, Juliet?" asked Delilah.

Miss Windermere nodded. "They're exploring the legend of the Centaur's Path."

No legend or myth in the world was safe from the Earl and Countess of Cumberland's indefatigable explorations. The *ton* viewed them and all their offspring as harmless eccentrics, but Rory saw the Windermeres for who they genuinely were— intrepid followers of their passions.

He admired that about them.

"Oh, my," said Mrs. Robertson around her spoonful of Scotch broth. "Wasn't your sister the one who married a duke?"

Delilah nodded. "The Duke of Ripon. The Duchess was safely delivered of a young future duke last year and has spent every waking hour since painting him from all conceivable angles."

Mrs. Dalhousie gave an approving nod. "And Lord Archer?" she asked. "Is he still on the Continent with his bride?"

"Indeed," said Delilah. "Who knows when they'll return to England."

Mrs. Robertson gave a censorious tsk. "To be away from one's homeland isn't natural."

Miss Windermere patted the corner of her mouth and set her napkin down. "Are you saying we Windermeres aren't natural?"

Silence descended on the room—even the servants stopped in their tracks—and Mrs. Robertson's mouth gaped slightly open.

Miss Windermere's disingenuous smile relented. "You wouldn't be the first."

Mr. Dalhousie barked out a jolly laugh, and relief broke the tension, giving everyone permission to enjoy the rest of the meal.

As conversation flowed around the room during the fish course, Rory found his gaze straying toward Miss Windermere more than once. He realized she'd always been like that. Not one to mince words, but to fearlessly speak the ones that cut directly to the heart of a matter. He also realized he'd always liked that about her.

"Lord Kilmuir," murmured Mrs. Robertson to his left, "would you mind very much passing the gravy dish?"

"With pleasure," said Rory. While the Dalhousies had serv- ants to attend to the meal, their suppers weren't such formal affairs that one didn't spoon a dollop of gravy onto one's own plate when warranted.

Without paying attention, he reached for the dish. But rather than encountering porcelain, he encountered…a finger.

His gaze cut over to find Miss Windermere's gloved forefinger just below his. Her gaze startled up, and she yanked her hand back.

It had been the lightest brush of fingers.

He should give a sheepish smile and dismiss the entire encounter as the sort of thing that happened at supper parties.

The contact was passing…insubstantial…inconsequential.

And yet…

It felt like the opposite.

It felt like it held substance…

Like there would be consequences.

And the look in Miss Windermere's eyes seemed to know it.

Chapter Two

IT WASN'T SIMPLY a touch of Kilmuir's long, masculine fingers that had Juliet snatching her hand back as if scorched.

It was the spark of something in his eyes…

Heat.

Directed at *her.*

Heat that flushed through her and sent her gaze skittering away.

She'd been determined to ignore his presence for the entire night—a particular skill she'd developed over the years—but it was an impossible feat when the blasted man was seated directly opposite her. And…

Touching her.

She shook the silly thought away.

He'd barely grazed her finger.

It was hardly of consequence that the point of contact still tingled.

Even as she sliced into a filet of trout, so too did the side of her eye cut in his direction. How was it possible that he'd only become more impossibly…oh, well, *everything*…since he'd moved to Scotland a year ago?

More impossibly broad of shoulder… More impossibly golden of hair… More impossibly bright of eye… More impossibly attractive, especially with his newly-grown, golden-red beard.

It was damnably irritating was what it was.

But, as in every other moment of her life, her natural reserve served her appropriately; her face maintaining its surface placidity so that her well of emotions could storm beneath.

That was what pen and paper were for, anyway. Pens quelled storms into manageable squalls that soon exhausted themselves on paper.

How she longed to jot down a few lines. But she supposed that would be considered rude and eccentric at a supper table where she was a guest of honor.

Juliet felt a gaze on the side of her face. From her place three seats down from Kilmuir, Delilah caught her eye. Her eyebrows lifted in silent question. Juliet gave her head a dismissive shake, unwilling to allow the slightest indication that anything was amiss.

"Now," said Mrs. Robertson, again directing her sharp gaze toward Delilah. Everyone asked their questions of Delilah first, which Juliet minded not in the least. It granted her opportunity for observation. "What brought you *unmarried*"—she gave her throat a light, prim clearing—"ladies all the way up to the Highlands, my dear?"

"It's a simple story, really," said Delilah, warming as she ever did to having all eyes upon her. "Our mother and Mrs. Dalhousie came out in the same London season and became fast friends."

Mrs. Dalhousie nodded wistfully. "What a wonderful time of life that was."

"And what brings you here now?" pressed Mrs. Robertson. Like all good gossips she had a nose for a story untold.

Delilah's gaze shifted to meet Juliet's. "Is it all right to say?"

Juliet nodded. After all, her enjoyment in committing words to paper was no great secret.

"Miss Windermere," said Delilah, "has become fascinated by a Scottish heroine of yours."

"Oh? Which one?"

"The warrior maiden, Scáthach of Skye," supplied Juliet. "Little more than research, really"

In fact, she was in the beginning stages of writing an epic poem, or possibly a play, about the female warrior. But she wasn't ready for that particular truth to be aired, so half of it would do for tonight.

"We decided she needs to stand where Scáthach stood," continued Delilah. "Breathe the air Scáthach breathed. That sort of thing. I'm not the creator of sentences here."

This was met with a small frisson of interest, but it passed quickly. "And Lord Kilmuir?" asked Mrs. Robertson, turning to her neighbor. The woman was determined to extract every morsel of gossip she could from this meal. "I noticed you weren't introduced to the young ladies. I take it you're already acquainted?"

"I know their brother Lord Archer from school," he replied. "We would see each other up here during term breaks."

Juliet remembered those wild barefoot summer visits well, as the Dalhousie estate neighbored Baile Ìm.

Delilah pointedly cleared her throat. Juliet detected an agenda in her cousin's eyes. "Now," began Delilah, "as it's nearly the thirtieth wedding anniversary of our outstanding hosts."

Mrs. Dalhousie blushed prettily, and Mr. Dalhousie smiled approvingly.

"I have a proposal for the gathered."

Juliet knew enough to brace herself, even as everyone else looked remarkably relaxed. They would learn.

"Let's put on a play."

A few beats of silence met the proposal. Delilah never could apprehend that most people would rather eat their left foot than tread the boards and spout lines from the Bard.

But Delilah was never one to allow a few beats of stunned silence deter her. "Shakespeare, methinks."

A low, pained groan caught Juliet's ear. She glanced across the table to find Kilmuir looking like he might, in fact, rather eat his left foot than have anything to do with this conversation.

And then Juliet remembered Kilmuir's full name. *Lord Rory Macbeth, the Viscount Kilmuir.* A bloodthirsty name, if there ever was one.

A few amused eyes cut in his direction, as surely he'd known they would. "How about the Scottish play, eh?"

A few laughs followed the *Macbeth* reference, and an unamused smile pulled at his mouth, which provoked a giggle from Juliet. It was likely wrong that his discomfort delighted her so.

His gaze landed on her and narrowed. "Or how about *Romeo and Juliet?*"

All eyes swung toward Juliet, and the laugh that had sprung from her mouth fell to the floor with a resounding thud.

Kilmuir heard it, for amusement shone in his eyes. He understood something about her most in this room didn't. Unlike her cousin, she didn't enjoy being the center of attention. Where Delilah blossomed, she wilted.

"No tragedies," said Delilah, unaware of the silent battle raging between her cousin and friend. "A comedy will do nicely. I was thinking *As You Like It.*"

At her end of the supper table, Mrs. Dalhousie brightened at the idea. "That would be a fun diversion, don't you agree, husband?" Mrs. Dalhousie never agreed to anything without her husband's express approval.

"I do believe you're right, my dear." And Mr. Dalhousie never denied his wife her heart's wish.

Mrs. Dalhousie's brow gathered. "But I do wonder if we have the numbers to fill out the play."

Delilah began explaining that they, indeed, did have plenty of actors. "I'll take on the role of Rosalind, of course, as I know all her lines."

"Dearest cousin," said Juliet, unable to resist a bit of teasing, "you know *all* the lines in the play. End of. You could perform it yourself in its entirety."

Delilah tapped forefinger to mouth, appearing to give the

idea serious thought, before shaking her head. "No, I think not. It would be better with a larger cast. Now where was I? Oh, yes, I'll play Rosalind, and Juliet will play Celia, of course."

Juliet nearly choked on the wine she'd been sipping. "*I?* I think not."

Delilah was the one who considered all the world her stage and Juliet the one who wanted nothing more than to write the lines.

"Well, I think you shall," said Delilah, firm. "And Miss Dalhousie can play Phoebe."

Miss Dalhousie gave her head a rueful shake. "I'm afraid I shall have to disappoint you, Lady Delilah."

"Oh?" Delilah wasn't accustomed to disappointment. She usually found a way around it. "Why is that?"

"A dear friend of mine has recently been delivered of her first child," said Miss Dalhousie, unperturbed, "and I shall be leaving tomorrow to pay her a visit."

Delilah flicked a dismissive wrist. "You'd only miss one day of rehearsal."

Again, that rueful, obstinate shake of Miss Dalhousie's head. "I shall be gone the week."

"But you'll return for the performance, dearest?" asked Mrs. Dalhousie.

Her daughter smiled her perfectly lovely smile. "I wouldn't miss it, Mama."

That seemed to satisfy all but Delilah, whose gaze was now casting about, taking in potential actors. "I suppose we can do it like in Shakespeare's day."

"And what way is that?" asked Mrs. Robertson.

"Use boys for the female roles."

That got a lift from more than a few sets of eyebrows. The numerous Dalhousie sons seated around the table didn't exactly accept the news with jubilation.

"Not I," said James, the eldest Dalhousie lad at around sixteen years of age. "I shall be Orlando."

Oliver Quincy, who had been—*blessedly*—quiet at his end of the table, laughed in his particular patronizing way. "You're a bit young for the role, don't you suppose?"

"I suppose no such thing," said James with no small amount of umbrage.

But Quincy appeared not to have heard him. "I shall be most pleased to offer my services for the role."

Of course, Quincy would want the part of Orlando. It would put him in close proximity to Delilah, who he'd been attempting to woo these last three years—to no avail.

It wasn't too difficult to see what was happening. Delilah was the prize for these two love rivals: Oliver Quincy, supercilious popinjay extraordinaire, and James Dalhousie, a besotted youth of sixteen years.

It should be an interesting week.

"I believe there is an ass in this play," said James, a mean glint in his eye. "There's a role that should suit you, Quincy."

Adults gasped; children snickered.

"Actually," said Quincy, undeterred. It was a known fact the man was impossible to insult. "I believe the character you're referring to is Bottom from *A Midsummer Night's Dream*."

"One thing is for certain," began James.

Quincy lifted a condescending eyebrow. "And what is that, young master?"

"He'll be Ass if you're playing him."

"James," interjected Mrs. Dalhousie, "I believe that's quite enough from you."

James crossed his arms over his chest and settled back in his chair, looking quite pleased with himself for having gotten in one final riposte.

"Mr. Quincy, you must accept our apology for James," said Mrs. Dalhousie. "He had a fever last week, and I'm afraid it might still be affecting his manners."

Quincy waved the apology off. "The delightful spontaneity of youth."

"And what about the rest of the actors?" asked an amused lady whose name Juliet couldn't recall.

Delilah gave a little shrug that said she already had the matter well in hand. "Kilmuir—"

His fork clattered to his plate. "What have I to do with the play?"

"You'll be in it, of course," said Delilah, certain. "With your acting skills, you would do nicely as..." She gave it some consideration. It was no secret that Kilmuir's acting skills, while earnest, lacked polish—to put it diplomatically. "We'll find something for you. Perhaps you can help construct the back-drops. Carpenters are always needed," she ended optimistically.

Juliet only just didn't snort as Delilah carried on assigning roles and deciding on a schedule while she consulted her pocket watch. She'd had pockets sewn into all her dresses so she could always have it on her person. Something about actors and timing, which went over everyone's heads, as she was the only Winder-mere with a capacity for, or interest in, keeping the time.

"It'll be too late to start tonight," said Delilah, "so we begin tomorrow. *Early*."

Beneath her lashes, Juliet's gaze slid across the table. Kilmuir had tucked into his cut of venison with the appropriate gusto for a man of his size and was now taking a gulp of wine. She followed the line of his gaze and found him looking down-table, in the direction of Miss Dalhousie.

Of course.

She still chafed at the idea of a resemblance between her and the other woman simply because they were both possessed of dark hair. Miss Dalhousie's luscious brown eyes were her most defining feature—eyes that were the opposite of Juliet's. Miss Dalhousie's eyes were the sort that invited one to fall in.

Further, Miss Dalhousie was quite an accomplished lady. She played violin with a level of mastery that spoke of many hours of devoted work. She painted and did needlework with elegance. She wrote in a flowery calligraphic script to rival that of a medieval monk. She even spoke French and Romanian. Apparently, the violin instructor had been from Romania. There was no end to Miss Dalhousie's accomplishments.

Juliet couldn't stand her.

Which she felt guilty about, because Miss Dalhousie—who on more than one occasion had implored Juliet to call her Davina—was an exceedingly agreeable person.

Who wouldn't be infatuated with her?

Yet… Why should Juliet care?

She harbored no more romantic illusions about Kilmuir.

The blasted man and Miss Dalhousie could have each other.

She stabbed a carrot with more force than necessary and brought it to her mouth.

It tasted like dust.

Besides, she had more pressing matters to consider.

Like how to make herself scarce on the morrow once Delilah began organizing the play.

Early.

Perhaps *early* would be a good time to make for the outdoors and start breathing some of Scáthach's air.

Chapter Three

Next day

JULIET SCRATCHED PENCIL against the blank white surface—and yet again it refused to march across paper and leave words in its wake in the usual fashion.

She let the pencil fall and cast her gaze about her surroundings. Beside her perch on a boulder of granite slipped a gentle stream as a forest of pines swayed in the light breeze. This should've been the perfect, idyllic spot upon which to receive inspiration. It was all here, and yet…

Somehow it wasn't.

She'd happened upon this particular curve of the stream on the far boundary of the Dalhousie lands in her escape from Delilah's exacting play direction. Juliet had taken a hasty tea before everyone else, grabbed her ready canvas bag filled with pencils and journals, and fled the house with no one the wiser. Best to stay clear of Delilah's path when she had a performance in her sights.

Juliet pulled out her copy of *As You Like It*. Before bed last night, Delilah had given firm instructions to waste no time in memorizing her lines. Juliet found it suspect that Delilah coincidentally happened to have brought twenty-one copies of the play all the way to Scotland—the exact number of speaking roles.

She gave a bemused shake of her head. In truth, she liked that quality about her cousin—her doggedness in pursuing her passions, even when that pursuit landed her in a hot bit of trouble. Like the trouble at Eton College that had landed them in Italy for several months, waiting out a scandal.

Not that Juliet had minded. Italy was lovely.

The breeze whispered through pine needles, and Juliet inhaled deeply of its crisp, earthy scent, a wisp of salt hidden within. No air in the world compared to the air of the Scottish Highlands—not even Italian air.

Much of what Delilah had said about their reasons for coming to Scotland was true. Juliet was here for research purposes. But there was more. She was here to get a feel for Scáthach herself. The way this land felt beneath her feet. The way this breeze felt in her hair.

She loosened her own hair from its single braid and allowed the breeze to take it. She removed her boots and slipped stockings down her legs, feeling slippery moss between her toes where rock met stream, cold Highland water rushing against her ankles. These elements shaped a person as surely as wind and rain shaped the face of a cliff. Nature and humankind were elementally linked, and ever would it be so.

And here in this Scottish wind and river and land would she find the elements that composed and forged Scáthach.

A frisson of anticipation skittered through her. Herein lay the elements that brought writing to life, and they were the only elements that made writing worth the effort of committing one's words, thoughts, and passions to paper.

A sudden rustling noise crashed through the not-too-distant brush. Juliet whipped around to find a great gray-and-white shaggy beast of the four-legged variety bounding straight for her. An inelegant "Ugh!" startled from her as she scuttled off the boulder in time for the dog to charge onto it and launch itself into the stream, where it began stomping and splashing in the water with the ease of familiarity.

"Clootie!" shouted a deep, booming voice.

Juliet knew that voice.

Through the woods emerged Clootie's owner—none other than Kilmuir. A great, shaggy owner for a great, shaggy dog. For Kilmuir was certainly shaggier than he'd been when last she'd seen him in London the previous year. And she couldn't help thinking the slightly longer hair that now curled at the ends and the dense golden beard cut close to his jaw and chin suited him perfectly.

Traitorous thought.

She caught the moment he noticed her. He gave his customary lopsided smile and wave of greeting. She returned the wave and offered a semblance of a smile. *Like for like… No more, no less.*

A furry head nudged her hand, and she glanced down to find Clootie staring up at her with a gift in her mouth. A river stone worn smooth. Juliet couldn't help but be charmed by the oversized collie. Then Clootie began shaking out her fur, thoroughly drenching Juliet in the lengthy process.

"You'll have to forgive Clootie her lack of manners," said Kilmuir, stepping within speaking range. "She's still a pup."

Juliet felt her eyebrows lift toward the forest canopy. "She must weigh four stone."

"Yeah, still a pup."

Juliet laughed. She found it impossible to be irritated by either pup or master. On this matter, at least. "Clootie?" she asked. The name hovered just beyond the reach of recognition. "What's a clootie?"

"A dumpling," he said simply.

"You named your dog after a dumpling?"

"Not just any dumpling," he said, his lopsided smile threatening, "but my favorite dumpling."

Irritatingly, Juliet found herself…charmed. "Do you venture to this part of the land often?" she asked. If the answer was yes, then she would find another contemplating spot. She wasn't sure how long her defenses could hold against being charmed by this man and his shaggy dog on a regular basis.

"Every morning, first thing." He jutted his chin toward Clootie. "This one needs a morning adventure or she gets up to mischief."

Juliet watched the collie chase a squirrel. "And she isn't getting up to mischief now?"

"Nay, she's just being a dog."

A short length of silence stretched out. "Is this not Dalhousie land?" she asked, searching for something of no particular importance to say.

"The stream is the border between our lands."

Ah.

And there was their paltry supply of small talk exhausted. Kilmuir shifted on his feet and looked suddenly uncomfortable. In fact, he looked like a man with something on his mind.

"In Italy," he began and let the words drift on the wind.

Juliet felt a flush begin in the center of her chest, heating her up by slow degrees. She didn't want to talk about Italy. Especially not with this man. Yet she found herself asking, "What about Italy?"

"In the olive grove," he began again. "Did I do something to cause you offense?"

Juliet pasted a false smile onto her mouth. "Of course not. You've always been most courteous."

His head remained slightly cocked to the side. He wasn't satisfied with that answer.

And why should he be? She was almost as terrible an actress as he was an actor, and she had no talent for false smiles.

She reached for her boots and hastily pulled them onto her feet. The stockings could wait until she arrived back at Dalhousie Manor. She grabbed her canvas bag, deciding now would be a good time to make her exit.

She gave Kilmuir a polite nod of farewell—her manners hadn't entirely deserted her—and pivoted on her heel. Clootie galloped to her side, demanding her own proper farewell as she placed her head beneath Juliet's hand. She stroked silky gray-and-white ears and muttered, "That's a good girl. Now you return to your master."

"Miss Windermere?" she heard at her back.

She'd ventured deep enough into the woods that she felt she could reasonably ignore Kilmuir. But curiosity, as usual, got the better of her, and she turned. "Yes?"

Kilmuir was holding a journal open in his hands, giving its contents a once-over. He glanced up, his eyebrows knitted together in mild bafflement. "Did you leave this?"

A thin ribbon of anxiety fluttered through her. Kilmuir was reading her words. "I did."

"Whose is it?"

"Mine."

A little frown turned down the corners of his mouth. "Yours?"

"It belongs to me."

"But—"

His eyes swiped across another page as if seeking some sort of confirmation. Juliet felt as if she were about to jump out of her skin.

His gaze lifted. "Who wrote it?"

A tick of time beat past as Juliet weighed the truth against a harmless lie. She was no good with lies, so the truth it would have to be. "Me."

His finger traced the paper as he read more. "A poet wrote this."

She watched the truth dawn across his too-handsome face.

"Miss Windermere," he began, stunned, "you're a poet."

Even as Juliet felt herself blush to the roots of her hair, a wave of gratification swept through her. Unlike practitioners of other arts, writers created in the isolation of their own minds, committing words to paper that might never be read—never even be acknowledged. But Kilmuir was reading her words with an expression of awe. Taking them in...acknowledging them...*enjoying* them.

Until this very moment, she'd thought it was enough to merely commit her words to paper. That therein lay the satisfaction. But now another view opened to her. That words on paper were merely their potential. To reach the fullness of their expression, another person had to experience them, and only then could the piece be complete.

And that it was Kilmuir reading and appreciating and enjoying her words felt better than good or gratifying.

It felt strangely—possibly irritatingly—*right*.

"YOU'RE MORE THAN a poet," said Rory, scanning line after line of perfect iambic pentameter. "You're a *good* poet."

He read more.

"An *excellent* poet."

Miss Windermere shifted on her feet. He was discomfiting her. But he couldn't tear his eyes away.

"You're the sort of poet anyone would want to be."

A wry laugh caught his ear. A laugh that indicated she didn't believe him. "I'm fairly certain not everyone wants to be a poet."

Rory's gaze narrowed on the woman before him. She was quite unlike the Miss Juliet Windermere he'd known for years, who viewed the world around her from a calm and deliberate remove.

This Miss Windermere looked a bundle of nerves.

He tapped forefinger to page. "I would give up quite a lot to be able to write words in the configurations you do. I'd give up my future earldom."

Her eyes twinkled with a suppressed smile. "But not your current viscountcy?"

She'd asked the question in all seriousness, yet he suspected she was teasing him.

He rather liked being on the receiving end of a tease from Miss Windermere.

"I'd prefer to keep it," he said. "I rather like Baile Ìm."

Her head canted to the side. "You do have a, erm, *way* with words."

Rory winced. If that wasn't damning by faint praise, he didn't know what was. "*You* have a way with words, Miss Windermere," he said, earnest.

He thumbed through the journal, each new page filled with more brilliance than the last.

Right.

He snapped it shut and held it out for her to take, only now realizing she hadn't given him permission to read her brilliant words. She stepped just close enough to grab it and took an immediate step back.

"My apologies for taking liberties with your work," he said, sheepish. It only seemed right.

She nodded her acceptance of his apology, but didn't turn to leave. "I've heard that you write the occasional verse."

"Very occasional," he said. "I've mostly stopped."

"Why would you do that?"

"May I be blunt?"

"I wouldn't have it any other way."

Oddly, he believed her. "I'm a bloody atrocious poet."

She smiled. "How can you know that?" she asked. "Have you shared your poems with anyone?"

"One person," he admitted. "One poem."

"Neither number is enough to gauge the quality of a work."

She'd asked for the truth. Here it was... "You know that I proposed marriage to Miss Dalhousie a few years ago?"

"I'd heard something about that."

"I wrote her a poem."

Miss Windermere gave a slow nod. "I take it the poem wasn't to her taste."

"The poem and I, as it turned out."

Curiosity lit within Miss Windermere's eyes. "Do you remember the first line?"

"I do."

"Would you mind reciting it to me?"

He considered saying no, but hadn't he just read her poetry without permission? Turnabout was only fair play. He cleared his throat. *"Ye are like a wee Highland coo, stout of mind, heart, and body."*

Brow lifted, mouth slightly agape, Miss Windermere looked utterly stricken.

Which was the same look that had come over Miss Dalhousie's face when he'd recited the line to her.

"You cannot say that to a woman."

"But it's the truth."

"No one wants to hear the truth about themselves."

"I wouldn't mind it." In fact, he'd rather like being compared to a Highland coo. He scratched his beard. He was well on his way, in fact.

"Allow me to clarify," Miss Windermere continued. "No *woman* wants to hear that particular truth spoken about *her*."

Rory pointed at the journal clutched to her chest. "See? If I had your way with words, Miss Dalhousie would've surely consented to be my wife."

It was only the truth—but a truth that held no bitterness for him. It was merely factual.

A funny look came over Miss Windermere's face. It was the exact same expression he'd once seen depicted on an Italian painting. The subject had been Joan of Arc.

He only just didn't take a step back.

"I could help you woo Miss Dalhousie," said Miss Windermere with the same note of fervency and inspiration that must've convinced thousands to follow Joan of Arc to their doom.

Rory spread his hands wide, hoping to calm this situation before it got out of hand. Fervent and inspired weren't his *métier*. "That will not be necessary, I can assure you."

He could tell even as he spoke them that his words landed on barren soil. "I can be your Cyrano de Bergerac," she continued.

"Cyrano de…*who*?"

"He was a French poet and adventurer a couple hundred years ago," she said, dismissive.

"And what has he to do with my situation?"

"He used his way with words to help others."

"And your way with words will help me how?"

"I shall write a poem for Miss Dalhousie, and you shall recite it to her."

Rory only just followed her logic. "So she would think the words mine, and…and *what* precisely?"

"Consent to be your bride."

Rory felt his brow gather. The fact was he hadn't considered trying to woo Miss Dalhousie again. She'd rejected his proposal, and he'd been cast down about it for a few months, but that had been the end of it.

Further, since becoming neighbors with the Dalhousies, he'd had opportunity to observe Miss Dalhousie more fully. She was kind and accomplished and very pretty, but upon reflection, whatever spark she held within her didn't call to a spark within him. That was the only way he could put it.

But Miss Windermere looked so strangely excited by the prospect of this poem that he was finding it difficult to deny her. She looked…*inspired*. And who was he to deny inspiration to a poetess of her talent?

"Oh," she exclaimed in a sudden burst. "I have it!"

"You have what?" he asked carefully. They always said artists contained a bit—or a great deal, in some cases—of madness in their souls.

"Miss Dalhousie will return in time for the play," she said, her words making sense only to her. "At the end, you can recite the poem to her in the audience."

"To Miss Dalhousie?" he asked slowly.

"It's perfect. It gives us one week—which is rushed for a finished poem—but it should be enough time."

"Hmm," was all Rory said. It would've been perfect two years ago, but now it felt decidedly less so.

Miss Windermere tapped a forefinger to her mouth, drawing Rory's gaze. Plump and pink. How had he never noticed that about her bottom lip?

"I do see one problem with the plan," she said.

Just the one? Rory didn't say.

"I don't really know anything about Miss Dalhousie."

"Well," began Rory, "she's an accomplished violinist and speaks more than a few languages, for starters."

Miss Windermere gave her head an impatient shake. "Not her accomplishments, but the true Miss Dalhousie." She pressed a palm to her chest, and Rory tried not to notice the shallow swell of her breasts beneath.

Truly, he did.

"*Here,*" she continued. "Her *true* life—the one that lives inside her heart."

In that instant Rory understood how Miss Windermere was able to write with the skill and emotion she did.

A poet's soul resided in her heart.

And he understood something else, too.

He wanted to know more of it.

An idea began to form. "She loves nature," he blurted.

"Oh?"

In truth, he hadn't the faintest clue. "I could show you her favorite places."

Actually, he was fairly certain Miss Dalhousie didn't enjoy being out of doors.

Miss Windermere gave a slow, considering nod. "That idea holds promise."

An unexpected flare of relief rippled through Rory. And it had naught to do with Miss Dalhousie, but with the woman before him clutching a journal of poetry to her chest and speaking of the truth that lived in a heart.

He now had the perfect excuse to spend time with her, show-ing her *his* favorite places, getting to know the true Miss

Windermere who resided in *her* heart.

Though he'd been acquainted with her for years—through youth and into adulthood—he was only now seeing her.

Today offered a glimpse, but tomorrow…

What new vistas awaited?

Yet a question did occur to him. "What benefit do you get out of this?" He simply didn't see it.

She blinked, and her straight black eyebrows drew together for a perplexed instant. They released. "To help a friend find his happily ever after, of course."

Rory wasn't sure if she believed the words as she spoke them, but he was certain he didn't. He and Miss Windermere had never been friends—or even particularly friendly.

However, he did think of a way to even the scales. "What can I do for you?"

"*You* do something for *me?*"

"It only seems gentlemanly."

"I'll, erm"—her teeth worried her plump bottom lip—"I'll think of something later."

Rory nodded. That would have to do for now. "May I escort you back to Dalhousie Manor?"

"I think not," said Miss Windermere.

"You won't get lost?"

"I never get lost."

She was sounding more like her usual, capable self, which should've been a relief. But he wasn't sure it was.

He rather liked the Miss Windermere who shifted on her feet and revealed more than she'd like to say. But he could see that Miss Windermere was lost to him for now.

He tipped his hat and whistled for Clootie before heading to his day's work.

More frothy bloat awaited.

He only just didn't groan aloud.

Chapter Four

Evening

"DELILAH, YOU'RE QUITE adept at controlling chaos, you know," observed Juliet over the rim of her teacup before taking a sip.

From the back of Dalhousie Manor's grand receiving hall, she and Delilah watched the space transform into an impromptu theater, the entire horde of Dalhousie lads, along with Oliver Quincy, springing to every whim and command that crossed Delilah's mind and lips.

In the short time since she and Delilah had sat to their tea, the dais that would serve as stage had been moved into place and the estate carpenter was presently hammering the final nail into the structure that would frame the playing space.

"One doesn't control chaos," replied Delilah. "One becomes one with it and merely"—she swayed her hands before her—"*influences* it."

A dry laugh escaped Juliet. "It helps when all those you command worship the very ground you walk upon."

Delilah bit into a slice of shortbread, even as her mouth twitched. "Yes, well, that does help." Her gaze landed on Juliet. "Have you memorized your lines yet, sweet Celia?"

Juliet had known this was coming. "Not quite."

"Oh, that's right. You enjoyed a ramble about the Dalhousie lands this morning."

Juliet shrugged. She knew better than to give ground when an imperious mood struck Delilah. "When given the two options, it's the choice I'll make ten of ten times."

Delilah released a long-suffering sigh, but Juliet knew that would be the end of it. No one ever met with much success in ordering Juliet about. "And how did you find your wanderings?" asked Delilah.

"Beautiful is too simple a word for Scotland."

"And Scáthach?" asked Delilah. "Did you receive inspiration for her?"

Juliet only just didn't snort. As an actress, Delilah felt all art to be divinely inspired, but as a writer, Juliet knew differently. Writing was one part inspiration and nine parts work. "I'm getting a feeling for her," she said simply.

Who was she to disabuse Delilah of her notions? To be the sort of actress Delilah wanted to be, she needed to believe in divine inspiration.

Delilah took a sip of her tea. "Anything of note occur?" Her eye caught on the stage, and she sat suddenly forward. Her teacup clattered onto the tabletop as she shot to her feet. "Mr. Quincy, if you would please set the hammer down and let Mr. Jones finish securing the frame..." Her voice trailed as she hurried down the center aisle toward the stage.

Leaving behind her question for Juliet.

Anything of note occur?

Oh, how to answer it...

A part of her—the part she held secret from all, including Delilah—instinctively knew she couldn't tell Delilah about seeing Kilmuir and his massive, shaggy dog.

Because then Delilah would ask what they'd talked about.

And there was no good answer for that.

For she herself could hardly countenance the direction their conversation had taken.

Actually, what she couldn't countenance was her boldness.

Had she, in fact, volunteered to write a love poem that

Kilmuir would use to woo Miss Dalhousie?

She'd taken leave of her senses.

Except that wasn't true either.

"What benefit do you get out of this?"

She hadn't told Kilmuir, of course, but she was very clear with herself about what precisely she *got* out of their arrangement.

She was helping him to help herself.

When viewed from that angle, what she was doing was incredibly selfish.

With Kilmuir happily settled with Miss Dalhousie, she would finally be free of the stubborn secret infatuation she'd been harboring for him all these years.

She'd thought herself free from it this last year, but that had been a delusion borne of necessity. Seeing him in all his shaggy, handsome Scottish glory last night—and again this morning—had only illustrated how wishful her thinking had been.

But it wasn't only his handsomeness that drew her—or even mostly his handsomeness.

He was kind and, most importantly, not vapid like so many thought him. He was able to see the simplicity in complex matters, which didn't make him a simpleton. It made him insightful.

And her poet's heart loved nothing more than simple language that could express complex emotion.

It took a special skill to take the complicated and make it plain.

Right.

Delilah returned, looking harried. "Controlling chaos isn't all sunshine and rainbows." She settled into her seat. "What were we talking about?"

Juliet shrugged and reached for her teacup without meeting her cousin's eye. If Delilah didn't remember of her own accord, she wasn't about to remind her.

"Oh, yes." Delilah canted her head at Juliet. *"Did* anything of note occur on your ramble?"

Blast. Delilah's curiosity was roused. Juliet gave her other shoulder a shrug. "If you count the flock of geese I happened upon who nearly gave me the scare of my life when they all took flight at once."

Actually, it had been wild and majestic and inspiring.

Delilah shot to her feet, again distracted by the stage construction—now it was the garland for the arbor that needed placing—giving Juliet a bit of room to breathe.

She and Delilah were close—they always had been and ever would be. Juliet had always sensed that the world saw them as two halves of the same whole, and growing up together close as twins, she had, too.

Until Rory had come along, and she'd become instantly besotted.

That feeling… She'd kept it to herself—*for* herself. If Delilah ever knew, she wouldn't be able to help involving herself—or inserting some mischief.

And that was the last thing Juliet wanted.

Movement caught the edge of her eye. Two men were crossing the threshold into the hall.

The Viscount Kilmuir and His Grace Sebastian Crewe, the Duke of Ravensworth.

Instinctively, Juliet leaned back, toward the wall—she was even tempted to slip behind the arras—for all their attention was fixed on the hullabaloo happening around the stage. Juliet couldn't quite make out the details, but Delilah's hands were on her hips and she was standing between a pugnacious James Dalhousie and a condescending Oliver Quincy.

Both Kilmuir and Ravensworth stood tall and broad of shoulder and too handsome for their own good. But that was where their similarities ended. Where Kilmuir radiated gold and light, Ravensworth possessed an altogether different mien with his dirty blond hair and light amber eyes that shone with intensity and purpose. Further, Ravensworth had always been supremely aware of his devastating good looks, while Kilmuir remained utterly indifferent to his.

Where Kilmuir viewed life from a place of clear simplicity, Ravensworth was…complex. A dangerous air had ever swirled about him, which some ladies—*many* ladies—found irresistible.

Not Juliet.

He simply wasn't the sort for her. She'd always known it instinctively.

And who was the sort for her?

Traitorous question.

Ravensworth's gaze had found Delilah. It was always where his eye went—directly to Delilah. Like a magnet.

A specific energy pulsed between those two. Yet Delilah couldn't stand to be in the same room with Ravensworth—not since the Eton scandal. Juliet had long sensed Ravensworth must've had a hand in it, but Delilah had revealed nothing.

Juliet wasn't the only one keeping secrets.

She felt the heat of a gaze on the side of her face.

Her eyes shifted, and the breath caught in her throat.

Kilmuir was staring at her. Inquisitive and insightful were those turquoise eyes.

Then he was walking…

Toward *her*.

This was…*new*.

And the feeling shimmering through her veins…

She wasn't sure she liked it. But one thing was almost certain.

She thought she might want more of it.

⚜

RORY WASN'T ABOUT to let Miss Windermere get away with that trick.

The one where she made herself invisible.

"Miss Windermere," he said. Her emerald eyes took on the hunted aspect of a trapped animal.

Ravensworth had no choice but to follow, though Rory could see he would prefer to make straight for Delilah. He didn't know what lay between those two, but they'd eventually sort it out.

They weren't his concern.

But the raven-haired woman in his sights somehow was.

"Kilmuir," she said. Her gaze shifted to Ravensworth. "Your Grace."

"Miss Windermere," said Ravensworth on a shallow bow. "What a delightful coincidence that you and Lady Delilah happen to be visiting Scotland when I happen to have business with Mr. Dalhousie. He's promised to invest in a concert pavilion in Glasgow, and I'm here to hold him to it." Ravensworth had a way of speaking utterly serious words in a light, offhand manner that fooled no one. Sebastian was a devoted patron of the arts.

A smile teased at the corners of Miss Windermere's mouth. "Oh, yes, quite a coincidence." It was clear she rather thought it wasn't.

A gruff laugh escaped Rory. He liked the way Miss Windermere didn't cede ground to a duke, even if that duke was one of his oldest friends. Sebastian could stand to be taken down a notch or two.

"Juliet," Delilah called out without looking in their direction. "Do you think Amelia would come up from London to paint the backdrop for the forest?"

"As she's six months gone with her second child—"

"She and Ripon are certainly good breeders," inserted Delilah.

"—the answer is no," finished Miss Windermere, firm and definite.

Delilah exhaled an irritated breath, but still she didn't glance up. "I need your opinion on the arbor, cousin."

"Perhaps Kilmuir or Ravensworth would like to offer their opinions, too."

Delilah's head whipped around. She gave their trio a quick once-over, her face transforming into thunder personified. Rory only just didn't laugh. He caught a twinkle in Miss Windermere's eyes. Pure mischief.

He hadn't known that about her.

What else didn't he know?

He would have a few opportunities to find out.

And he was rather looking forward to them.

Delilah strode up the center aisle, a rose in one hand and a peony in the other. She looked determined to ignore Ravensworth as she asked her cousin, "Which do you prefer for the arbor?"

It was Ravensworth who answered. "I think roses particularly suit you."

Delilah inhaled sharply, as if bracing herself for a deeply unpleasant thirty seconds, and faced Ravensworth. She couldn't ignore him forever. "And why is that?"

A sardonic smile curled along one side of his mouth. "They have thorns."

"Peonies it is," said Delilah.

Ravensworth swept his arm around. "What's all this, anyway?" Before anyone could reply, he answered his own question. "A play." He snorted. "Of course."

Delilah crossed her arms over her chest, and her jaw clenched. She wouldn't be answering. That was apparent.

"It is, indeed, a play," replied Miss Windermere.

"And what play would that be?" asked Ravensworth.

"As You Like It."

His smile widened. "Two cousins venturing into the forest to make a bit of mischief," he said. "Sounds like two cousins I know."

"How long will you be staying at Dalhousie Manor, Your Grace?" asked Miss Windermere.

"Oh, I'd say a week or so."

A look settled on Miss Windermere's face—like the cat who had got the cream. "We could use some help in making up the number of players. Perhaps Ravensworth would like to take a role?"

All the color drained from Delilah's face.

Rory saw that poetry wasn't Miss Windermere's only skill. That ability might just be rivaled by her ability to wind her cousin up.

"If Ravensworth stays," said Delilah, "we'll need to change the play."

"To *The Taming of the Shrew*, perhaps?" asked Ravensworth.

"I'm thinking *Julius Caesar*."

"Quite a few stabbings in that one, if memory serves."

"Precisely."

Ravensworth snorted.

"Have we settled on an Orlando yet?" asked Miss Windermere.

Masterful, that question. For Rosalind was the lead of the play, and Orlando was her lover.

"Ravensworth can*not* be Orlando," said Lady Delilah, decided.

"Why not?" asked Ravensworth.

"Because *I* am Orlando."

They all four turned to find James Dalhousie standing with his hands on his hips, chest puffed out like a lizard who wanted to make himself look more menacing to his enemies. Someday, the lad would make a formidable man. Today wasn't that day.

Ravensworth squinted. "Has your first chin hair even sprouted?"

"That's correct," Delilah said quickly. "James has already been given the role of Orlando." One couldn't help but notice the air of relief hanging about her. She cast a dismissive glance toward Ravensworth. "You can be Duke Frederick."

A frown formed about his mouth. "The villain?"

Delilah shrugged, clearly pleased with herself for having finally got a point on the board. "If the doublet fits."

Rory cleared his throat. This would be a good time to quell the sniping between Delilah and Ravensworth. He pointed toward the stage. "I see everything is in place." That was him relieved of carpentry duties.

Miss Windermere met his eye. She saw what he'd done, and approved. He wasn't sure why the notion made his body heat up a few degrees.

"Our gracious hosts already had a dais for our use," she said. "It was simply a matter of getting the stage into place and constructing a frame for it."

"Juliet—" began Delilah.

How had Rory never noticed what a lovely name Juliet was? Or that it perfectly fit Miss Windermere?

"Roses or peonies?" Delilah finished. It was clear the only opinion that mattered was her cousin's. These two had ever been so.

Yet something more Rory found himself liking about Miss Windermere. While she might tease and wind her cousin up, there was no question where her loyalties lay.

"Peonies," said Miss Windermere—*Juliet*.

Delilah let the rose drop to the table. "Will you arrange a section of the garland like usual?"

Rory followed the direction of the cousins' gazes and settled on the length of greenery twined around the top beam of the stage frame. His eyebrows creased together. "How exactly is Miss Windermere supposed to arrange the garland?" he found himself asking.

Delilah stared at him as if he were the dullest block of wood. "With a ladder, of course."

"It's a good twelve feet high," he pointed out. Someone had to be the voice of reason with the Windermeres.

Miss Windermere shrugged. "Nothing I haven't done before."

"I...I..." Rory found himself saying. "*Forbid it*," he didn't say.

Three sets of curious eyes landed on him. Delilah's brow had lifted. Ravensworth's eyes had narrowed. And a little frown was pulling at the corners of Miss Windermere's mouth, as if she'd intuited the completion of his unfinished lordly command.

"I...I shall lend my assistance," he stated. He didn't ask.

"You mustn't worry, Rory," said Delilah. "Juliet has a talent for flower arranging and general greenery placement."

As if artfully arranged flowers were any concern of his.

Truly, the Windermere genius lay in utterly ignoring a point when it didn't suit their ends.

Miss Windermere plucked the peony from Delilah's hand and strode toward the stage. She was a tall woman, with long legs beneath those white muslin skirts. When she walked decisively fast, she strode.

He rather liked that about her, too.

He found himself following slowly, feeling in no small part a fool, his eye never wavering from her as she directed a middle Dalhousie lad—*Ned*, this one was called—to place a ladder at the center of the stage by leaning it against the upper frame. She grabbed a handful of white peonies from the wicker basket at the base of the ladder.

A feeling churned inside Rory's stomach. He didn't much like where this was headed. For if his hunch was correct, Miss Windermere intended to—

Peony stems tucked into the pink sash at her waist, freeing up her hands, she placed one hand, then the other, onto the ladder and began climbing. No one seemed to take notice or be particularly bothered, least of all the lady herself.

Add fearless to Miss Windermere's vast intelligence and massive talent.

In combination with her good looks, she might be the perfect woman.

Now, where had that thought come from?

Rory found himself standing at the base of the ladder. "Should you be going up quite so high?" he called up.

She glanced down. "How else am I to place the flowers?"

One could hardly challenge the logic of the question, but... "Do *you* have to be the one placing the flowers?"

She tossed him an irritated glance. "Yes." A beat. "If you're going to insist on standing there, you can make yourself useful."

"How's that?" he asked. Neck craned, he grabbed the base of the ladder with both hands. She'd climbed up to the second highest rung.

Also, there was the matter of her skirts.

Namely, it would take hardly a shift of the eye to see up them.

He wouldn't…

He couldn't.

A cold sweat sheened his skin.

If he were to ever see up her skirts, it would be by permission.

Hers.

Definitely not at the behest of the cockstand that was beginning to form inside his trousers.

He must think about something—*anything*—so as not to make an even bigger fool of himself than he was already.

"Grab the basket of peonies," she said. "I'd like to arrange a three-foot section to get an idea of how many we'll need on performance night."

He wanted to tell her *no* in no uncertain terms, but he also wanted to be involved. For it was very clear that if he didn't do as she asked then she would simply ask someone else. A spare Dalhousie lad would happily volunteer, no doubt. And Rory needed to be close in case—*when*—something happened.

In silence, they worked together as Rory handed up one peony after another, Miss Windermere taking them. It was with no small amount of relief that he handed her the final flower. All she had to do was stick it in the garland and descend.

But with the final peony, Miss Windermere miscalculated and stretched her arm a hair too far, her weight tipping left and making the ladder wobble to one side. Luckily, Rory had just returned both hands to the ladder and was able to tighten his grip and steady it.

A nervous, little laugh escaped Miss Windermere. No small

amount of relief in that laugh.

Unluckily, she overcompensated to the right and tilted off-balance entirely, tumbling off the ladder and falling—

Into arms Rory only just got into cradling position in the nick of time.

He was no small man, but his knees nearly buckled beneath him when the full force of her weight hit. Though tall and willowy, Miss Windermere didn't lack substance.

Warm body snugged against him, face inches from his, he met her direct emerald gaze. His lungs forgot how to breathe and his heart forgot how to beat and the Earth might've forgot how to turn on its axis.

Her hair had come loose from its knot at the base of her neck and now spilled over her shoulders in waves of black silk, releasing a scent of sage and jasmine. Miss Windermere's scent, he now knew.

What intriguing intimacies she'd unwittingly shared with him—the scent of her…the feel of her.

He'd been holding her for a few ticks of time too long.

But he didn't seem to know how to stop, for she felt…*right*…in his arms.

Then Delilah was there, and he was releasing Miss Windermere.

Physically.

The memory of her wouldn't be so easily surrendered.

He found himself talking, his voice a gruff approximation of itself. "Shall I collect you here on the morrow for our, erm, wander-about? Ten of the clock?"

"Or," she began, "perhaps it would be easier for your morning duties if I meet you at Baile Ìm around midday tea?"

He nodded. That was most considerate of her.

Delilah's eyebrows crinkled so deeply on her forehead, they might've left a permanent indentation. "*Wander-about? What wander-about?*"

"Kilmuir has volunteered to show me places similar to those

Scáthach would've experienced," Miss Windermere lied, cool.

"Did he?" This from Ravensworth, who was watching the proceedings with entirely too much knowing in his eyes.

But the man didn't know anything, and Rory intended to keep it that way.

Whatever was happening between him and Miss Windermere…

He felt oddly protective of it.

And he had a feeling it wouldn't bear up against too much scrutiny.

It was time to leave. But he had one more thing to say to Miss Windermere. "You'll not be placing any more flowers today, correct?"

She drew herself up to her full height. "As it happens, I shall not."

He nodded. "I'm off."

"I'll take that as my cue, as well," said Ravensworth.

Both men pivoted on their respective heels and didn't speak again until they were outside beneath a sky just beginning to accept the idea that it would have to turn into night eventually.

"Where are we going?" asked Ravensworth. The man might rub some people up the wrong way with his dukely imperative, but those people didn't know him for the friend Rory knew him to be. Sebastian was loyal and protective, almost to a fault.

"To find the nearest loch to jump into."

A laugh rumbled at his side. "Can't think of a better idea."

Leaving Dalhousie Manor, Rory knew three things more than he had when he'd entered.

He knew the scent of Miss Windermere.

He knew the feel of her.

And he knew that even the frigid waters of a Scottish loch in April wouldn't be enough to wash the scent and feel of her off his skin.

Chapter Five

Next day

FROM HER TIME spent here in youth, Juliet knew the Scottish sun to be a stingy one.

But not today.

Today it poured its light and warmth freely onto all who would venture beneath its yellow rays for a ramble about this wild, beautiful land.

As she took the two stairs up the stile gate, stepped over the top rail, and descended on the other side, moving from Dalhousie to Kilmuir land, a sort of freedom took hold of her. Here, alone in a field of wild buttercups, thistle, poppies, and broom, she was free of obligation to anyone or anything but her own senses. She was free to form her own impressions of field and sky. Their colors filling her eyes. Their soft, sometimes rough, textures brushing along the tips of her fingers. Their crisp, earthy scents filling her nose, her lungs. The distant whistle of a lark or *baa* of a sheep providing a song for her ears.

These elements filled her heart and her soul, gave them width and depth and vastness. *Nourishment.* That was what Scotland gave her.

She topped a hill, and her feet had no choice but to stop, her hand held to her forehead. That view…

In the distance below stretched Baile Ìm. The manor house was composed of gray granite in the ornate style that had been popular in the last century. With its pair of turrets flanking the front entrance, steep pitched roof, and dormer windows, it was a structure meant to impress. Beyond it lay a narrow loch that ran into low hills that shone green, brown, and gold in the sun.

Figures bustled below—men, women, animals. Baile Ìm was a working estate, lest she forget. She experienced a surge of appreciation for Kilmuir, and what he was seeking to accomplish here. A year ago, he'd left London to immerse himself in something that mattered…something that lasted.

Just as words on paper lasted, so, too, did this.

Kilmuir didn't know it, but he was making a poetry of his own here.

She followed a trail that wound through a small copse of birches, their canopy verdant green against their slender silvery trunks, and opened onto the side of the manor house that led to its outbuildings. The farmyard should have been mostly empty as everyone would've been tucked into their midday tea. Instead, she found it a frenzied hive of workers shouting and charging about. Even Clootie had joined in the ruckus, barking and racing to and fro.

A quick assessment revealed that a sow had escaped her pen with her piglets, who were presently squealing and streaking across the farmyard as everyone gave chase. It didn't take long for her to pick out Kilmuir's head of auburn hair amongst those scrambling about.

A little pink fellow with floppy black ears broke free from the group and began racing toward Juliet, his eyes wild at the prospect of freedom in the woods beyond. "Oh, no you don't," she said as he attempted to streak past her. She reached down and scooped up the naughty piglet who was writhing and squealing in her grasp as if she'd stuck him with a pin. "I shall call you Shakespeare, as drama appears to be your forte," she said on a laugh.

"I've been told not to name the animals," came a deep familiar voice to her left.

Juliet pivoted to find Kilmuir striding toward her with an armful of squirmy piglets and a golden lock flopped across his forehead. He was in quite the disheveled state, but entirely unbothered by it. No dandy was Kilmuir. In fact, somehow, in plain wool working clothes he managed to look entirely himself.

Over the squealing, he continued. "Naming them makes it harder for what comes later."

"Ah." Juliet preferred not to think on that. Still, she might pass on the pork at supper.

Kilmuir jutted his chin toward the nearest barn. Three of his men had managed to capture the sow with a noose around her neck, but she didn't appear too inclined to follow the lead as she planted all four hooves and shifted her weight against her would-be captors. With one worker to either side of her rump, they each dug a shoulder in and shoved with all their might, pushing and cajoling her into a stall, one laborious inch at a time. At last, it was one final nudge, and she was inside. Kilmuir and Juliet bent over the pen gate and returned her piglets—the happy family reunited and free to plot their next escape.

Outside the barn, Kilmuir dusted his hands off on his trousers, his head shaking with bemusement. "That was completely unanticipated."

"Life on a farm, I suppose."

He gave a wry laugh of agreement. "I might need to change my clothes, or risk smelling of piglet on our ramble this after-noon."

"I don't mind," said Juliet. And strangely—surprisingly—she didn't.

His brow gathered for an instant and released. She'd surprised him, too. "Even so," he said, "a quick wash at the yard pump wouldn't go amiss."

Juliet glanced at her own hands coated in piglet grime. "You're likely right about that."

Kilmuir took hold of the handle and said, "You'll want to stand back a few more feet. When the water comes, it's a gusher."

He gave a forceful heave of the handle, and the water did, indeed, slosh out in a great wave, coating not only Juliet's hands but her spencer nearly up to her armpits. She jumped back on a startled laugh. "Now, it's your turn."

She took hold of the handle and gave it her all, but only a trickle of water poured forth. "Hey!" she groused.

Kilmuir rubbed his hands together beneath the measly trickle of water. "It's enough, lass."

Something occurred inside Juliet.

Lass.

She liked being called lass.

By him.

"One more pump," he said.

Juliet did as instructed. Another measly trickle of water.

Kilmuir removed his red kerchief and wet it before swiping it along the back of his neck. A few beads of water escaped down his clavicle, trailing down the open V of his shirt.

Oh.

Her eyes should lift. They should dart away and take in any number of the happenings around her—Clootie nuzzling her hand for a stroke, a maid hauling a bucket of milk from a barn... She could even count the individual stones of Baile Ìm. But her eyes refused to tear themselves away from the man before her, and the bead of water that led the gaze down... A hint of muscle—muscle whose solid steel she'd experienced yesterday when he'd caught her—a fuzz of golden hair...

As if the force of her gaze had the power to will his shirt away, she stared. A sudden and ferocious desire to see more—*all*—made the breath catch in her chest. Surely, the bead of water had reached his stomach...the waistband of his trousers...and below that...

Oh.

So, this was what lust felt like.

Her infatuation for this man seemed to have entered a new

phase.

A throat cleared.

His throat.

Her gaze startled up.

"Are you ready for our afternoon explorations?" he asked, his gaze giving nothing away.

"Erm"—she cleared her throat—"yes."

He grabbed a knapsack and tossed it over his shoulder. "Provisions."

She nodded and gathered herself. She was known for her composure. She wouldn't let it fail her now as she fell into step—not behind him, but not exactly beside him either—as he led her into the Scottish wilderness.

Well, not precisely the wilderness. Not yet, anyway. For now, they were cutting across fields of his land. Some fields were used for crops, and others for animals, mostly sheep. Yet others lay fallow. They'd made it to the middle of one such field when a loud *moo* sounded.

Kilmuir came to a sudden stop, causing Juliet to stumble over her feet. "What is it?" she asked, low, feeling the whisper warranted for some reason.

"It was a mistake to cross this field," he said.

Juliet glanced about. All she saw was tall grass with a few poppies scattered about. "It's a lovely field."

But Kilmuir hadn't taken his eyes off an object in the distance. He pointed, and Juliet looked to find a shaggy red, rather massive, Highland coo watching them. If an animal could wear a grumpy expression on its face, this one did.

"This wee fellow has gotten quarrelsome in his old age," muttered Kilmuir.

The coo stamped a hoof as if to illustrate the point.

"See the kissing gate behind me?" Kilmuir asked in a level tone. The sort of tone that wouldn't further irritate a grouchy Highland coo who was now shaking his head.

Juliet craned her neck and found the gate. "Aye."

"Walk toward it slowly—no running—and don't stop until you're through and in the next field."

"What about you?" Juliet wasn't going anywhere until he explained that.

"Hamish's grievance is with the world in general, not me in particular," said Kilmuir. "He's losing his sight, but he knows my voice. What he wants is a song."

"A song?"

"Just do as I ask, if you will." Kilmuir's voice brooked no opposition. She'd never heard that tone of voice from him.

Commanding.

She rather liked it.

She'd entered the simple maze of the kissing gate when she heard it—a deep, masculine voice lifted in song. She turned and found Kilmuir approaching Hamish, who had canted his head slightly to the side. The coo had settled. She knew not the words Kilmuir sang, for they were in Gaelic, but she thought it was about the sweetest tune she'd ever heard.

Kilmuir ruffled the beast's fur when he finished the song. Hamish then followed him to the kissing gate. Juliet stood back, while man and beast bid one another farewell.

Once they resumed their walk, Juliet said, "I haven't any notion of what you were singing, but it was a lovely song. A lullaby, was it?"

"Aye, *Cagaran Gaoloch*. It's his favorite song."

"What does that translate to?"

"*Beloved Little Darling*," said Kilmuir with a sheepish smile.

"I can see *beloved*, perhaps, but *little...darling*?" A laugh escaped Juliet. "That might be stretching the facts."

"I was assuring him that he will grow into a brave, strong lad who will steal goats, horses, and sheep for the good of his clan."

Juliet couldn't stop smiling. "And how did you come by the knowledge that it's his favorite song?" They'd come this far; she must know.

"I've known Hamish since the moment of his birth. His mama died a few days later, so I helped bottle feed him until a cow could be found to take him. I would sing to him then."

"That is so incredibly"—there was no other word for it—"*sweet.*"

Twin flames of scarlet lit the tips of Kilmuir's ears in the way that could afflict those with red in their hair.

She'd made him blush.

Well, that was rather sweet, too.

He cleared his throat. "We'll be following the trail for about twenty minutes."

"Twenty minutes?" said Juliet, surprised. "And this is one of Miss Dalhousie's favorite places?" She enjoyed being out of doors as much as the next lady, but twenty minutes into the wilds of Scotland might be a touch farther than she would've expected Miss Dalhousie ever to venture.

"Mm-hmm," was all the reply that sounded over Kilmuir's shoulder.

They ascended a slow-rising hillock and began following a stream. Juliet let the Highland environs drift through her senses even as her gaze remained steadily fixed on the man in front of her. From an artist's point of view, he was quite sturdily built.

An artist's?

Hardly.

Not one of her more poetic observations. The man wasn't a thick-trunked tree, after all.

Then the view before them opened, and all such hackneyed observations faded into irrelevance. The relevant point was, before them, a waterfall had appeared as if by magic. From a hundred feet above, it poured down in three distinct tiers into a small pool that flowed into the stream they'd been following all this time.

Juliet wasn't one given to loud exclamations when overcome with delight. Instead, she preferred to find a place to sit—as she did now—and quietly take it all in. The first word that came to mind was usually the most banal word, and this waterfall and the entire surrounding tableau of moss-covered rock, mist-clouded air, and leaf-dappled bluebird sky high above deserved better.

Kilmuir took a seat a few boulders over. He didn't rush in with a bevy of observations, but rather took in the view alongside her for a long while before asking a question. "How would you describe this waterfall?"

She understood he wasn't asking for the thoughts of Miss Windermere the lady, but rather Miss Windermere the poet. "I would find a single word and create from there."

"What single word comes to you now?"

"Sublime."

"That's a good one."

"It's a start, but it doesn't actually say anything about the waterfall itself. It only really describes my feeling about the waterfall."

He snorted, drawing her gaze. "How would you describe it, Kilmuir?"

Like for like.

"*Pretty.* That's what I would say about this waterfall. Then I would find a word that rhymes with waterfall."

Juliet canted her head. This was becoming strangely interesting. She'd never spoken with anyone about the process that happened before words were committed to page. It only followed that every individual's would be different. "And what word is that?"

Kilmuir tapped a pensive forefinger against his mouth. "*Eyeball?*"

A sudden laugh slipped from behind Juliet's hand. "Forgive me, but—" Along came another laugh that wanted to be a howl. "Please lead me through that succession of word choices."

"It's simple. You see the waterfall with your eyeball."

"True," she said, slowly. Her mind cast about for another word. "Perhaps *enthrall?*"

"See?" He pointed at her.

"See what?"

"Right there," he said. "That's what you can do that I cannot."

Juliet felt the compliment down to her bones. But there was a misconception she wanted to clarify. "Of course, you can. Everyone has expression inside them that's bursting for release. But sometimes it requires a bit of digging to get to it."

"That's assuming we all have the same depths, Miss Windermere. Perhaps some possess more than others."

Juliet couldn't deny that fact, but she also knew something else. They hadn't yet scratched the surface of Kilmuir's depths. "But what else is the waterfall?" she asked. "What is it beyond a pretty pleasure for the, erm, eyeballs?"

"*Wet*," he said. "I would say it's wet."

"Water isn't actually wet. That which it touches is."

Kilmuir's eyebrows drew together and released. "I've never met anyone like you, Miss Windermere."

"*Met?*" she scoffed. "We've known each other for well over a decade."

"But why is it I feel like I'm only now meeting you?"

Juliet didn't have a ready answer for him, or, at least, not one that would do. What she did have was a flush of heat suffusing her body, making her shrug off her pelisse.

"Here's what I want to know," he continued. "How do you arrive at what *you* would say?"

Juliet felt on safer ground here. "I start by looking for the essence of the thing. What are the elements that compose it? Then I think about how it makes me feel. What and who I am in relation to it."

"Show me the waterfall as you see it."

Like that, the conversation turned from the theoretical into the intimate. These feelings… She was accustomed to expressing them on paper—not aloud to another living soul.

And yet…

It felt safe with Kilmuir.

He wouldn't make light of what she expressed.

In fact, she wasn't sure she'd ever felt safer with another person than she did in this moment with him.

Chapter Six

RORY THOUGHT MISS Windermere might not answer.

It would be her artistic prerogative, after all.

Then she opened her locket and slid out a small pencil and a few scraps of paper. She began writing as she spoke, and her words flowed over him as smoothly as the water over centuries-worn river stone. "A series of impressions will come to me. Sometimes one word or two. No longer than three. Usually adjectives of the senses—sight, smell, hearing, taste, feel. But that is the effect on me. The essence of the thing must also come through. What is it elementally at its core? Not how I feel about it, but what is its intrinsic value? And once I arrive there, then I can begin to form a narrative around it."

Rory had never heard anyone talk about writing or words or images or feelings the way she did—like she took them to heart.

Here sat a different Miss Juliet Windermere from the one he'd assumed her all these years.

Here was the artist.

And yet she spoke to him as one artist to another, as if they were on an equal plane, though he knew the opposite to be true.

He was a terrible poet.

He'd long known it.

But he loved it.

Yet the poetess before him knew and didn't care. It was as if they met not in talent, but in a passion of the mind, and that was enough for her.

She turned and fixed her ardent emerald gaze upon him. She'd always shimmered with intensity, Miss Windermere. He'd always assumed her intensity was something he didn't want to get mixed up in. But now, after coming to know her, he was seeing it from a new angle.

"By coming here and experiencing this place that Miss Dalhousie loves," she said. "I shall be able to begin forming a narrative about her."

Miss Dalhousie… Rory hadn't given the lady a moment's thought. But that wasn't what Miss Windermere assumed.

Right.

Perhaps Miss Dalhousie wasn't the best excuse to spend time with Miss Windermere.

"And you," she continued.

"And *me?*"

"Certainly." She swept her arm around. "For you admire the woman who admires all this."

"*You* admire all this, don't you?"

Miss Windermere's brow gathered in bemusement. "I do," she said slowly.

Rory opened his mouth to say that, aye, he did admire the woman who admired all this, and that woman wasn't Miss Dalhousie. But then he noticed something above his head. The sky, namely. It was transforming into an ominous shade of purplish-slate.

He slung his knapsack over his shoulder and shot to his feet. "If we start now, we might make it back to Baile Ìm before the storm breaks."

"Storm?" Miss Windermere tipped her face toward the sky. A fat droplet of rain landed on her nose. "Oh."

The wind chose that moment to start blowing.

She pushed to her feet and scrambled to follow him. "Do you

think we have twenty minutes?" she called out to his back.

"It's all downhill," he tossed over his shoulder. "We can make it in ten."

But eight minutes later, the sky decided the time had arrived to relieve itself of its burden, and unloaded a torrent of rain onto their heads. Rory reached back. "Take my hand," he yelled. "I know a place nearby."

A rapid beat of the heart later her cold, wet hand slipped into his, and he tightened his grip around it, careful not to lose her. Within thirty seconds, they were shoving beneath an old lean-to shelter that needed a good tearing-down, though he was thankful for it today—even with its roof that leaked and absence of walls to protect them from the wind.

Instinctively, they huddled close to the old oak that provided the lean-to's only reliable support.

With not a foot of space separating them, it occurred to Rory that he'd never stood this close to Miss Windermere.

No, that wasn't true.

Yesterday, he'd caught her in his arms, giving him a feel for the substance of her body.

And today, she'd given him a feel for the substance of her mind.

And each only made him want to know more of both.

She lifted her hand and, before he knew what she was about, she'd swiped a layer of rainwater off his cheek. "See? My hand is wet." She smiled. "*You* are wet."

A laugh roared out of him. He lifted a sodden clump of hair that had escaped her chignon. "*You* are a sopping wet mess, Miss Windermere."

And the laugh that sprang from her was pure joy to his ears. A messy Miss Windermere—so opposite her usual poised and perfect self—was a sight he'd pay to see.

"Can I offer you my greatcoat?" he asked.

"My pelisse is sufficient."

His eyes narrowed on her. He should've expected that reply.

"What is it?" she asked.

"Your lips are taking on a hue of lavender."

A smile quirked about her purplish lips. "And how does that make you feel?"

A tick of time beat by before they burst into laughter. But in the next instant, Rory felt himself turn serious.

He knew exactly how it made him feel.

Before his mind caught up with what his hand was doing, he was reaching out and cupping the nape of her neck, his other hand sliding around to the small of her back, drawing her into the warmth of his open greatcoat. Her face tipped up, and eyes clear as green ocean glass met his.

"It makes me feel like warming them up," he muttered into the space between their mouths.

"And how would you go about that?" she asked, her whisper glancing across his lips.

"Like *this*."

His mouth brushed against hers, a first touch, their lips slick against each other. Suggestive, that slipperiness. The hand at her back tightened and gathered her closer, so the slender length of her body met his, allowing not even a sliver of air between them. Her arms reached up and circled his neck, and he felt the hard buds of her breasts against his chest. The kiss had no choice but to deepen as his tongue sought hers. A surprised gasp escaped her, but she caught on as her tongue ventured to touch and tangle with his.

This was her first kiss.

He was her first kiss.

And, strangely, it felt right to kiss this woman he'd never once considered kissing in all the time he'd known her.

As if some part of him had been biding its time for this very moment.

His fingers found themselves trailing down the indent of her lower back to the curve of her sweet, round bottom. Her hands contained a certainty of their own as they roamed across his chest and around to his back, and lower to give his arse a responding squeeze.

"Like for like," she muttered against his mouth, a sly smile pulling about her lips.

Oh, that smile sent his mind to places his body wanted to go. Places that wanted—*demanded*—satisfaction. Satisfaction he couldn't give. For his instinct was to seize control, as was his wont when he was alone with a willing woman.

But this woman in his arms was no bit of crumpet for whom he would provide an afternoon's pleasure.

She was a lady.

A lady who happened to be a cousin of his closest friend and who, in truth, was more like a sister of the Windermere brood.

Right.

His mouth broke from hers, intent on doing the noble thing.

Which was to stop kissing her.

Still, she remained within the circle of his arms, mouth parted, panting, cheeks flushed, eyebrows drawn together in question. "Was it terrible?" she asked.

Oh, he was but a mere, weak, mortal man, and he couldn't have Miss Windermere distressed or thinking she was terrible at anything.

Before he could talk himself out of it, he claimed her mouth again, this time with a sense of desperation. With a responding desperation, she pressed all her weight into him, so he was left with no option but to follow her lead until his back hit solid oak.

Miss Windermere seemed to know what she wanted.

And it seemed to be him.

His half-full cock went suddenly as hard as the oak at his back.

Her hands trailed lower, guided by a frenzied curiosity, and anticipation filled him to bursting. He knew what those inquisitive fingers would find.

Him.

Tentatively, they grazed along the rigid length of his shaft, pulling a long groan from him. Serious green eyes met his.

"*Again*," he rasped. He would beg if he had to.

She held his gaze and stroked him again, applying more pressure this time. As the flame of need licked at him, he understood there were only two directions this could go.

He could swivel them around so it was her back against the tree, bunch up her skirts, wrap a leg around his waist, and release his cock. He could tup her silly right here. It was the satisfaction his body demanded.

Or…

There was another option.

He could stop.

Right.

It was the only option.

He pulled back, tearing his mouth from hers, and took her waist in his hands, gently setting her a foot away from him. They stood apart, panting, staring at each other, trying to grasp what exactly had just happened. She opened her mouth to ask the question he could see poised on her lips. He held up a hand to stop it.

"You are not terrible at kissing," he said.

"Then why—"

"You know why, Miss Windermere."

Surely, she did. Him kissing her and cupping her firm, round bottom. Her caressing his full-to-bursting cock. Them going at each other against a tree…

It was all wrong.

She was a relation of his closest friend.

And she was a virgin.

He was no despoiler of virgins.

The question left her eyes. "I see."

Of a sudden, she was no longer the Miss Windermere he'd been kissing seconds ago, but rather the Miss Windermere he'd known all these years—cool, collected, and not particularly impressed by him.

Clearly, he'd done something wrong.

But he couldn't think of what—for he'd done the right thing.

He supposed doing right could be wrong under certain circumstances.

Although Miss Windermere looked in no mood to enlighten him.

She stepped to the edge of the lean-to, stuck her head out, and peered up at the sky. "Looks like the rain has let up."

Thunder rumbled in the distance. "But not for long," said Rory, shedding his greatcoat. "Take this."

"But I—"

"*Take it.*" She wasn't the only one with a stubborn streak.

She did as told.

"If we leg it," he said, joining her at the edge of the leaky roof, "we can make it to Baile Ìm before the next round of storms start up."

He didn't have to tell her twice as she hitched up her skirts to her knees and streaked across the field.

As he followed, and kept his eyes fast on her, he could hardly countenance the Miss Juliet Windermere who had revealed herself to him these last few days.

She wasn't at all the person he'd assumed her all these years.

He wanted to know more of her.

And he would.

Chapter Seven

Five hours later

JULIET STOOD BEFORE the guest bedroom's bow window and stared out across Loch Ìm toward hills golden-hued with spring buttercups. Though it was nearly eight at night, the April light had done naught more than cast a gray evening haze. The gloaming, the Scottish called it.

The rain hadn't let up, rendering the fields boggy and the road connecting Baile Ìm to Dalhousie Manor impassable. She would be staying the night.

Beneath Kilmuir's roof.

The very idea defied belief.

She turned and took in the bedroom. Clean, but out of current fashion in the manner of a place benignly neglected. Like the atmosphere outside, this room held a gray haze, but it was from the lack of a woman's touch.

Also benignly neglected? The dress she was wearing.

While her garments dried before the fire, a cheery maid had rummaged through an old cedar chest and at the bottom had found this dress, which was surely more than twice Juliet's age. Thankfully, she was a good eight inches taller than its original owner, so the hem cleared the floorboards by a few inches, rendering panniers unnecessary. All she needed to complete her impersonation of a high-born lady from the previous century was a towering white powdered wig and a beauty patch on her right cheek.

She took a seat before the dressing table and began to twist her hair into a simple chignon at the nape of her neck. She caught her eye in the mirror. The image before her was identical to the one she'd known all her life, and yet…

Who was she?

Who was the woman who nearly ravished a man because he was too polite to refuse her kiss?

For that was what had happened this afternoon in the rain: a near ravishment.

By her.

Of him.

But, oh, his kiss—and the hot, solid feel of him beneath her fingertips—had been everything her secret dreams had thought it would be.

The kiss had started sweetly enough. But when his large, sure hand had trailed down her body to cup her bottom before dragging her against his, oh, so *hard* length, some mechanism flipped inside her. With his massive, muscled body, he became an object of lust, and she'd become ravenous for him.

Then, like that, he'd pulled away.

"You know why, Miss Windermere."

Her jaw clenched.

She did.

Miss Dalhousie was why. Though absent, her presence never hovered too far away.

Juliet's cheeks should be burning with mortification, but they refused.

Thwarted was closer to how she felt.

"Milady?"

Juliet swiveled on the low stool to find the maid at the door. "Yes?" Though not technically a lady, in this servant's eyes she was.

"I'm to lead ye through the house to supper."

Juliet stood and gathered a soft woolen shawl about her

shoulders. This plain gray garment would never be worn to dine in London. But the Scottish had a much more practical outlook, a fact that didn't go unappreciated.

As Juliet was led to the dining room, she couldn't help noting how very different this house was from Dalhousie Manor. All dark mahogany wainscoting and sparsely lit wall sconces, this house was shadowy and spare, not an ounce of fancy or whim on it—a bachelor's residence.

If anyone in London discovered that she was spending the night alone with the eminently eligible bachelor, the Viscount Kilmuir—never mind the ten or so servants also inhabiting the place—her reputation would be shredded to tatters.

But this was Scotland, and those rules felt very far away.

As if they didn't apply to her here.

She touched a fingertip to her lips. They were still swollen from the intensity of the kiss...from the delicious scrape of his beard.

She hoped the feeling never faded.

She entered the dining room and found Kilmuir rising to his feet—as a gentleman should—at the other end of a long, oval table gleaming with the reflected glow of flickering light from the candelabras placed along the perimeter of the room. The crystal chandelier above remained unlit, for which she was grateful. It would've made the dinner feel formal. She much preferred this cozy feel.

Her gaze met his. A taut silence stretched long, and, of a sudden, the twenty feet between them was nothing.

The kiss... It was here.

The knowledge of it.

The remembered feel of it.

A feel that hadn't left her lips...

Or her hands from touching his body...

From touching...

Him.

A feel that had her squeezing her thighs together beneath her skirts.

For the place that corresponded with *him* was still begging for a touch of *her* own.

"You look…" he began, clearly searching for words.

Juliet plucked at her skirts. "Like your grandmother?"

He snorted. "Hardly."

"Like your grandmother's ghost?"

He cocked his head.

"The dress, my lord," she said, answering his unspoken question. "It was in fashion when Marie Antoinette yet remained in possession of her head."

"Ah," he said, resuming his seat when she took hers. "I don't go in for lady's fashions."

"I should hope not," she said. "The empire waist wouldn't suit you."

He gave a dry laugh. "And here it is."

"Here *what* is?"

"The renowned wit of Miss Windermere."

The remark wasn't in the least caustic, but spoken with that too-appealing lopsided smile of his. He wasn't the least intimidated by her wit, that smile said.

She liked that about him.

His solid, quiet confidence.

Oh, she more than liked it. She found it…*ravishing*.

"We shall have to shout our conversation all night if we keep these places at the table," she said.

He nodded. "Perhaps we meet halfway?"

In unison, they rose, and she went to her left, and he to his, so they now faced each other across the crosswise span of the table.

"Better?" he asked, sitting back as servants moved their table settings before them.

"Much."

His scent reached her here. Kilmuir always managed to smell like man, but somehow like good man. A man who had hiked three hours in a pine forest and perhaps rubbed a bit of sap on himself for good measure. She was never been able to smell pine without thinking of him.

A bowl of soup appeared before her, and her heart lifted. "Cock-a-leekie," she said, lifting a spoonful to her mouth.

"It's mostly simple fare we eat here," said Kilmuir.

"I look forward to my trips to Scotland just for the soup."

They each tucked into the meal before Juliet supposed she should be a good guest and make conversation with the lord—or in this case *laird*—of the manor. It was odd to think of him in that way. It seemed so…*adult*…which could be a strange thing when they'd known each other since youth. And yet… "In the year that you've been here, you seem to have settled into the running of Baile Ìm," she observed.

She wouldn't observe—at least not aloud—that it imbued him with a new seriousness and capability that only enhanced his manly attractiveness.

She cleared her throat. "Do you enjoy it?"

"Aye," he said, taking a draw of his ale. "You know Archie is like a brother to me."

She nodded.

"But around the time I turned thirty, I'd grown tired of playing the spoiled lord about Town."

She felt her brow lift. "You and Archie were very popular. Particularly amongst the ladies."

He snorted. "Lords are always popular amongst ladies."

"You're referring to title huntresses," she said. "But you and Archie aren't exactly toads." He had to have an inkling what supremely dashing figures he and Archie had cut in those Mayfair drawing rooms.

He shrugged the observation away. "Well, it was boring."

And there it was—that ability of his she so admired. To take a complicated matter and make it simple. Because the simple truth was Mayfair drawing rooms *were* boring.

The idea occurred to her that she hoped never to return to one.

Ridiculous idea.

Of course, she would. She was an unmarried lady who made her home in London. Those drawing rooms were an integral part of her life there.

"And are you ever bored here?" she prompted. She wanted to know more about his life in Scotland.

"Never. I might even be somewhat useful." He sat back and let a servant take his empty bowl. "Or at least, that's my goal. My tenants and workers might not think so yet, but I'm determined they will."

Before she knew it, honest words were spilling from her mouth. "I think you can do anything you put your mind to." *Too honest.*

A note of surprise flashed behind his eyes before a mischievous light replaced it. "Even write poetry like you?"

"Perhaps not that." She wouldn't let him change the subject. "But that doesn't mean much. Simply our talents lie in different directions."

"Diplomatic of you to say."

"I never say anything I don't mean, Kilmuir."

His head cocked to the side. "Is that true?"

"Yes," she said, feeling less certain of the statement than she had a moment ago. He had the look of a man about to use it to his advantage.

"I have a question for you then."

She hesitated. "And that is?"

"Out of all your family, you're the only one who never called me Rory."

Her mouth snapped shut.

"Why is that?" he pressed.

Her heart beat out a heavy thud. She'd just told him she never lied, but to tell the truth after all these years…

And yet why shouldn't she?

She reached for her tankard of ale and took a long pull. She released a small burp behind her hand before saying in a rush,

"The answer is quite simple." She inhaled a quick, bracing gulp of air. "I harbored a—"

"A hearty distaste for the lumbering Scottish brute Archie was always bringing home during holidays?" he inserted with a smile that now reached both sides of his mouth.

Oh, that she could speak around this lump in her throat… "I harbored a secret infatuation for you."

His smile froze, and the room went airless in the wake of her secret exposed. Into the stunned silence, she added, "In my youth."

"*Infatuation?*" he repeated. "For *me?*"

She nodded, tightly. So many feelings charged through her—mortification, bafflement…relief. Strange, that last one.

At last, he spoke. "I thought you could barely tolerate my presence."

"I…I couldn't." Now, she would have to explain. "Because of the infatuation." She shook her head. "It was complicated."

"And *that* was why you didn't call me Rory?"

"Mm-hmm," was all she could get out.

His head cocked to the side, watching her with utter and complete concentration. "And now?"

"*Now?*"

Oh, what new mess had she landed in? How could she explain how she felt about him now when she didn't understand it herself?

"Why don't you call me Rory *now?*"

Oh. She'd spoken of her infatuation in the past tense. There might yet be a way out of this mess… "Erm," she said, her mind racing. "Habit."

His eyes narrowed on her. "Well, you're not an old dog, are you?"

"Erm, no," she said, trying to understand what he was about. "If I were a dog, I would be quite an aged one at three and twenty years of age."

He smiled, but that discerning look hadn't left his eyes. "But you're not a dog, Miss Windermere."

She sat perplexed and silent. One could take a multitude of meanings from that statement.

"And you can learn new tricks."

Ah.

"Call me Rory."

It was an invitation. It was a command. One she couldn't—didn't want to—refuse. The invitation warmed, but the command and the intent in his eyes when he spoke it lit dark and secret places inside her into flame.

Servants chose that moment to enter the room carrying several large plates laden with the heartiest meal Juliet had ever been served—an entire filet of salmon, leg of lamb, boiled, smashed potatoes, turnips, and haggis. No proper Scottish meal would've been complete without haggis.

"This is quite too much for me to eat, Kil—"

He glanced up and pierced her with his opaque turquoise gaze.

"*Rory,*" she finished. In truth, she quite liked his given name.

"What we don't eat tonight will be finished on the morrow."

"That's practical of you."

"Have you ever met an impractical Scotsman?"

"I reckon not." She'd taken only a few bites when she found him staring at her. "What is it?"

"Scáthach," he said. "What made you think to write a poem about her?"

"I've been intrigued since I first heard the mythology about her as a child."

"Tell me."

Again, a command from him.

And again, a response from her body.

"Her name translates to The Shadow," she began. "That was what first sparked my interest. I'd never heard a woman described so." She took a forkful of salmon that melted in her mouth. "Then there's the legend itself. She lived with her daughter

Uathach in a fortress on the Isle of Skye."

"Have you ever been to Skye?"

Juliet shook her head. "I hope to someday."

"You would love it there. Perhaps we could visit." A beat. "Together." His eyebrows crinkled. "With Delilah accompanying us, of course."

"Of course." Juliet cleared her throat. "And Scáthach trained warriors. Not female warriors like the Amazons, but male warriors. She also invented a weapon. A barbed harpoon called Gáe Bulg. But the mythology has always treated her as a mere stopping point for the real heroes of the story."

Rory poured a glaze of sauce over his turnips and haggis. "Didn't she train Cú Chulainn?"

"My point exactly," said Juliet. "He began an affair with her daughter Uathach, but when he injured her—"

"Injured her?"

"It was apparently an accident that he broke her fingers."

"Broke her fingers? And this fellow who broke the bones of women became a hero?"

Juliet had never seen Kilmuir—*Rory*—look so thunderous. She continued, "In pain, Uathach called out for her other lover—"

A hearty laugh erupted from Rory.

"—Who Cú Chulainn dispatched there and then. Feeling guilty about the whole situation, Cú Chulainn indentured himself to Scáthach and promised to marry Uathach."

"What a gentleman," said Rory, dry.

"A promise he didn't keep." She shrugged. "But, really, my interest doesn't lie with Cú Chulainn, but rather with Scáthach, and her ability to maintain autonomy in a world dominated by powerful men. To become a powerful woman in her own right, she sometimes had to use those men to achieve her own ends. For example, she had Cú Chulainn defeat her sworn enemy, who also happened to be a powerful woman—some say Scáthach and Aífe were sisters—which is yet another avenue to explore."

"And that avenue is?" Rory seemed genuinely interested.

"The ways powerful women can become pitted against one another in a patriarchal society, which only serves to benefit and uphold that system."

Rory nodded. "Sounds like you have quite a bit of story to tell there."

Juliet felt her adamancy give way to a smile. "Indeed."

"Your poetry has purpose to it."

A blush crept through Juliet. She could think of no higher praise. "I can't imagine you give a fig about anything I've had to say."

"Would you like to quiz me?" he asked. "I was never any good at school, but I would pass your test."

The intensity of his gaze was almost too much.

She wanted to look away.

She didn't want to look away.

No one turned her into a bundle of contradictions like this man.

A laugh wrapped in nerves escaped her parted mouth. A laugh full of bravado. "Because, of course, you've been hanging on my every word," she said, cool and distant, because that was the sort of witty repartee expected from Miss Juliet Windermere.

Rory didn't flinch or seem particularly impressed or amused by it. "Yes."

Her mouth snapped shut.

All her wit and sophistication and cartload of words that could run around in circles for days had no defense against this—Rory's straightforward honesty.

Chapter Eight

RORY SETTLED BACK in his chair and watched Miss Winder-mere—*Juliet.*

He supposed if she could call him Rory, then he could, at least, think of her as Juliet.

Like for like.

Wasn't that what she'd said against his mouth earlier?

His *yes* had thrown her off balance. *Good.* He supposed she could stand to be set on the back foot once every so often.

But, oh, what a raven-haired beauty she was tonight in her passion and fervor.

"You're glowing," he said.

"Perhaps I've caught a fever."

He cocked his head. "You have a ready response for every occasion, don't you?"

"Most."

He understood something. His direct gaze unsettled her.

Further, he might like that.

She glanced around as if something only now occurred to her. "Where is Clootie?"

"She prefers to sleep in the stables and keep an eye out."

"Good girl."

"Aye."

He liked that she asked after his dog. It spoke well of a woman who liked a man's dog.

Looking at her now, tucking into her haggis, he couldn't help observing how she looked in this room—in his house.

So natural.

So *right*.

Servants began clearing plates, replacing them with two glasses and a bottle of whisky. Rory nodded and said, "That will be all for the night."

Alone in the room with Juliet, he poured them each a dram. "Have you tasted Scotch whisky?"

Her nose looked as if it wanted to wrinkle. "I have."

"Try this one. We have a small still on the estate."

She took a testing sip. "It's…earthy."

"Prefer wine, do you?"

"I think I do," she confessed. "The ale is nice, too."

As they sat across from each other, her usually direct gaze avoided his as she fidgeted with the whisky tumbler. He realized he needed to say something to her. It should've been the first sentence out of his mouth the moment she'd entered the room. "I must offer my apology for—"

Eyes clear with certainty lifted. "The kiss."

"Aye."

She canted her head. "Why should you apologize?"

He blinked.

"We both know I enjoyed it." A shy smile curled about her mouth, yet the words spoken were so…*bold*. "And we both know you enjoyed it, too."

His cockstand. She was referring to the cockstand she'd stroked through his trousers.

Thankfully, she didn't know about the one presently lifting its head.

If ever a woman could give him a cockstand with her words, she would be Miss Juliet Windermere.

Still, she needed to be set straight. "Our mutual enjoyment of the kiss is beside the point. We shouldn't have kissed in the first place."

"Why shouldn't we?"

The woman was stubborn on a point, he would give her that. In case he ever doubted she was a true Windermere.

She spread her hands wide. "You and I are full-fledged adults. We are free to make our own decisions."

"It was ungentlemanly." He could hold to a point, too.

"My kiss was freely given. Are you apologizing because I actually was terrible at it and you wouldn't want to do it again?"

This woman might be the death of him.

"No…no, of course not. In fact, it was the best—" He clamped his mouth shut.

"The best what?"

"The best kiss of my life."

There, he'd said out loud what he'd been avoiding admitting to himself.

Her eyes narrowed. "It was the only kiss of mine, so I have nothing to judge it against."

"You can trust me," he grumbled. "It was an excellent kiss."

"I'll take your word for it."

Irritation spiked through him. "Will I have to kiss you again to prove it?"

Now it was her who wasn't flinching. "Perhaps."

Of a sudden, she pushed away from the table and stood. For a moment, he thought she might flee the room. But, no, Miss Juliet Windermere was made of sterner stuff. She didn't flee provocative conversations; she provoked them further.

With a sure step, she made her way around the table, and he turned sideways in his chair so he could appreciate her approach. A feeling settled in his gut—and lower, too.

A feeling of anticipation.

A feeling of certainty.

She would have her way.

And he would have his way with her.

Nay.

They would have their way with each other.

She came to a halt not a foot away, staring down at him, wild daring in her eyes.

And a promise, too.

The promise that whatever he wanted, she would give.

One had to be careful with such promises. One must respect them. For this promise, it was precious, and it was his duty to protect it. To protect *her*—even from herself.

"And how did the kiss make you *feel*?" she asked, a smile tickling about her soft pink lips.

Just as Rory began to answer, the joke caught up with him. He chuckled. She could be quite funny. And yet…

He wanted to answer the question.

"It made me feel all lit up inside."

Her gaze grew serious. "We'll make a poet of you yet."

"All I need is the right inspiration."

A long moment passed. It was all he could do not to reach out and pull her toward him. This afternoon had only been enough to whet an appetite, not satisfy it.

"Would you do it again?" she asked.

"What would you like me to do again?"

He was evading. He knew *what*.

"Kiss me."

Rory had a choice here.

To kiss or not to kiss.

There would be no going back from a second kiss.

But, at this moment, with her body so close and the intent in her eyes so clear, he wasn't sure why he would ever want to.

"Yes," he growled as he caught the nape of her neck and pulled her toward him.

A FRISSON OF triumph sparked through Juliet.

But that wasn't all she felt—or even mostly.

What she felt as her body swayed forward and her lips met his was a desire so strong it made her trembly in ways she'd never experienced or expected.

The press of his lips was firm and the taste of his mouth sweet and earthy from the whisky as, testingly, she darted her tongue inside.

His large hands spanned her waist, and for the first time in her life, she felt small. She'd always been tall—taller than all the boys as a girl and most men as a woman. She'd always liked the feeling, in truth. But here, with this man, she liked this small feeling, too.

The afternoon's kiss had felt like pent-up release. But here, now, she went slower, took her time to savor him—his scent, his taste, his touch—though all the same urgency from earlier flowed through her, demanding she follow this path to surrender—hers...and his.

He groaned into her mouth and tugged her waist. Swaying forward, she stepped between his parted thighs, his massive hand on the curve of her lower back, snugging her tight against him. Her body became a molten version of itself against his unyielding solidity.

"Rory," she spoke against his mouth.

His eyes slitted open, those turquoise depths opaque with desire.

"I need you," she whispered.

It was the only way, she saw.

She would go mad from unrequited lust if she didn't have him.

For to have him was the only way she could let go of him.

An upside-down logic, but it held fast.

But the next instant she saw she'd approached it all wrong, for he was—for the second time today—wrenching his mouth from hers and setting her physically away from him.

But this time, unlike earlier, she planted her feet and refused to cede ground.

His head tipped back so he could hold her gaze, he said, "That should've put your mind at ease as to your, erm, kissing abilities."

"Perhaps, but…"

"But?"

"But not other, erm, parts of me."

For a woman known for her words, she was having remarkable difficulty conveying them. But what were words to *this*—desire…ache…craving…*feeling*…

This was all that mattered.

This was everything.

He gave his head a slow shake. "You mustn't say such things out loud."

"Who are you trying to convince? Me? Or…" Without precisely planning to, she reached for his cravat. "Yourself?"

"You're provoking temptation, Juliet." His voice was the consistency of crushed velvet.

Her hands began to work the knot. "And temptation leads to…" she trailed. White silk released, and his shirt flopped open, revealing the hard throb of his pulse against the base of his throat. "If this were a poem," she continued, "what word would rhyme with *temptation*?"

Consummation, neither of them needed to say.

She took the two ends of his cravat in one hand and gathered her skirts with the other. She hardly knew herself. Yet…

She couldn't think of a time when she'd been *more* herself.

Bundle of contradictions, indeed.

"Would you do more?"

"*More?*" he rumbled, the syllable naught more than a scrape against his throat.

With measured calculation, she placed one leg, then the other, over his muscled thighs. Of a sudden, the intimate air between their mouths was the only air capable of giving her life. "*More*," she whispered, the word brushing across his lips.

They both knew what more. It was there in the word left unspoken.

Consummation.

"After I agreed to be your Cyrano and write a poem for Miss Dalhousie," she continued, "you asked if there was anything you could do for me."

"You were to tell me later."

She'd gone far.

Too far.

Too far to turn back now.

"I've thought of the something later."

"Miss Windermere—"

"*Juliet,*" she said. "I want you to call me Juliet."

"Juliet—"

"And I want you to make love to me."

"No," he said simply, certainly.

She was only now seeing how his uncomplicated way of viewing the world could present a problem.

"You're a virgin," he continued. "You will marry someday."

She pulled back, but didn't move off him. And he made no move to make her. In fact, his hands were on her waist, steadying her so she wouldn't fall.

He would never let her fall.

He'd already proven it once.

But she had him here, finally. "I shall not marry."

"You certainly shall."

Her reasons had long been clear in her mind. "I'm an heiress who doesn't need a husband. I can make my own rules."

He snorted, dismissive. "You Windermeres." He shook his head. "You all think that."

"But we can," she said, undeterred. "And we do."

"And yet here you sit, straddling"—a crack in his voice released on the word—"me without having followed through on your own logic."

"Pardon?" she asked, indignation building. She very well

might've shot to her feet if his hands hadn't been holding her firmly in place.

"It's simple," he continued, evenly. "If anyone were to find out about us as we are now, you would have to marry." A ragged heartbeat of time ticked past. *"Me."* Another beat. "Would you risk your freedom for that future?"

Yes.

But how to say it without sounding positively desperate for him.

The fact was she'd risk anything for him in this moment of absolute, aching *need*.

Even forever.

She pressed her mouth against his ear. "No one will ever know," she cooed into the intimate space. "It'll just be this one night."

His jaw clenched as if he were waging silent battle with himself.

No matter.

She would win the war.

And the part of herself that had nothing to do with the mind, but only with *feeling* intuited exactly how.

Chapter Nine

JULIET REPLACED HER lips with her tongue and stroked along the whorl of Rory's ear, dragging a long, ragged groan from him.

That groan made her toes curl inside her borrowed slippers.

Of a sudden, his arms tightened around her and he stood. "If we're going to do this—"

"Oh, we most certainly are," she assured him.

"Then we shall do it properly," he finished. "In a bed."

And with that, he marched with her in his arms straight through the dining room and down corridors blessedly empty of servants, until he was pushing open a door with his shoulder and depositing her to her feet on a worn wool rug before a low fire in the hearth.

"The bed is over there." She indicated the rather imposing four-poster draped in heavy, satchel-brown velvet draperies from the same century as her dress.

"I didn't want to be presumptuous."

"I quite insist you presume."

"This is your last chance."

She shook her head. "This is *your* last chance."

As they stood facing one another, her gaze dipped to the outline of his cockstand clearly illuminated by the flickering light of the fire. A shiver of desire rippled through her.

Perhaps it was her last chance.

Her last chance to have exactly what she wanted.

This man.

On what could only have been characterized as a low growl, he reached out and caressed her cheek before running his fingers along the nape of her neck. With a few quick movements, her hair was tumbling about her shoulders and down her back.

The dark intention in his eyes... Gone was the light-hearted Rory and in his place was a man whose utter command of the moment sent lightning to hidden places only he could touch.

If his gaze could do all that, what more could his body do?

His hand continued to trail down the column of her neck...along the line of her clavicle...lower still to the small mound of a breast, fingertips grazing a hardened nipple through fabric. She gasped.

A wicked smile tipped at his mouth. "You like that, do you?"

"Yes," she rasped. Only the truth would get her what she wanted.

More of his touch.

A chuckle rumbled deep in his chest as he pulled her to him. His head lowered, her parted mouth angled up, and their lips met. And all the while, his fingers hadn't left her nipples—far from it. They'd slid beneath her bodice and were now squeezing the hardened tips, pleasure blazing through her to unexpected places, encouraging a wildness inside her.

Her hands raked through his hair, grabbing hold as she pressed up against the long, thick mass of his body. His body, however, wasn't the only long and thick part of him. His manhood was certainly making its presence known.

But, oh, his kiss... The way his firm mouth claimed hers possessed a force behind it, but not too much force. A drive...a will... The same drive and will demanding she follow this path where it led. She couldn't become lost, for she was with him.

He pulled back. Her eyes startled open, indignation flaring through her. "You haven't my permission to—"

"Shh." He placed a quieting finger over her mouth. She might feel indignant about that, too. "Trust me."

She searched his eyes and found utter confidence there. She nodded.

A flash of a wicked smile, and he took her hips in hand and swiveled her around. Of a sudden, she felt vulnerable and strangely exposed, though she remained clothed. There was a tug on her dress, then another. He was untying the laces. Then he was pushing the garment down her body, leaving her clothed in naught more than chemise, stockings, and slippers.

"No corset?"

"One wasn't necessary."

Next the thin muslin of her chemise was sliding up her body. Instinctively, she lifted her arms to allow it over her head, her hair following before succumbing to gravity, the ends meeting the upper curve of her derrière with a swish. She might've heard another growl. Then his hands were on her lower back, nudging her forward—toward the bed.

Once she reached it, his hand fell away. "Do you still trust me?"

"Entirely."

He pushed her hair to the side and kissed the nape of her neck, his breath warm and humid. Goose bumps raced across her skin, lifting the fine hairs of her arms, tightening her nipples into hard buds.

His presence, behind her, felt sensual…and slightly wicked…

She felt a kiss lower, and lower still, his hands clutching her hips, steadying her, as he trailed kisses down her spine. She tipped forward to brace herself on the bed and a chuckle sounded. "You naughty lass."

And it occurred to her: Lord Rory Macbeth, the Viscount Kilmuir, the nicest man she knew, had a penchant for wickedness.

In the bedroom.

To quote him, the realization made her feel all lit up inside.

She could be her most wicked self with him.

The idea appealed, even as she felt vulnerable and exposed.

Another contradictory bundle.

He cupped her bottom, taking a cheek in each hand. "You have the sweetest round arse in all Creation." He kissed one cheek, then the other. Down legs gone trembly with desire his kisses trailed. Every touch of his lips sent twin shivers of pleasure and ache rioting through her. She wanted this—his mouth…his large, capable hands…upon her—but she wanted *more*, somehow.

She squeezed her thighs together.

"Yearning for it, are you?" he spoke against the back of one knee.

She glanced over her shoulder. What she found in his eyes stopped the breath in her lungs.

Desire and determination writ plain.

He wanted her, and he would have her.

It was a promise.

"Yes," she said on a whisper that sounded more like a plea.

"Spread your legs."

She inhaled a gasp. The very idea seemed slightly transgressive.

But wasn't she in this room to experience exactly that?

A little bit of wickedness…a little bit of transgression.

She did as instructed, the ache of desire that had become centered in her sex now a heavy throb. Whatever he was about to do next… She wanted it.

She would perish without it.

Then she felt it…a slow, calloused stroke along her slit—his rough finger a delicious glide across her sex, lighting up every nerve ending in its path, pulling from her the longest moan of her life. She collapsed onto her forearms, no longer able to support herself as pleasure streaked through her. His other hand pushed at the small of her back, encouraging an arch, surely revealing more of her sex to him. *Wicked.* He stroked her again. "Oh, Rory," she groaned, hoarse with utter need.

A pressure pushed at the entrance of her sex. His long, thick finger... It was entering her. Another new sensation...another one she couldn't live without.

Slowly, deliberately, he moved, in and out of her, and a feeling began to build. All those lit-up nerve endings clamored for *more*—with every movement of his fingers...every kiss of his mouth which had, oh, wickedly, joined his finger...his tongue touching her in places she'd never imagined tongues could go. Those nerve endings gathered in purpose, increasing her pleasure with his every movement until she was naught more than a panting, groaning vessel enslaved to the sensation only he could provide.

And that building feeling in her sex... Oh, it had her in its grip as she strained toward a place beyond her experience or imagining.

His finger slid from her, and his mouth pulled away, and she cried out, "What are you about, Rory?" It was a question, a plea, and a demand.

He chuckled and turned her around. She collapsed onto the bed and, across the naked length of her body that was both enervated and clamoring for more, she watched him discard one article of clothing after another with smooth efficiency.

"Patience, my pet." He unbuttoned the fall of his trousers. "I'll get you there."

He tossed the garment aside, and here he was—naked, every inch of him hard and unyielding and beautiful.

Italian statuary had in no way prepared her for this: a flesh and blood man with a look in his eye that said—*promised*—he would devour her whole.

And she would enjoy it.

My pet?

She reckoned she was.

Her gaze roved across him—shoulders...chest...stomach bulked with muscle...the red-gold dusting of hair that narrowed on its descent toward...*him*—his manhood. So long and thick and *ready*. Like the rest of him, it was beautiful, too.

Her mouth went dry.

But other parts of her, well, they'd gone decidedly *wet*.

Commanding and sure, he grabbed her thighs and stepped between them.

"How is that going to fit?" It was only half a joke.

The lopsided smile that curved about his mouth lost its boyishness. It was all determined man. "You'll find out." His grip tightened on her thighs, and he pulled so her bottom reached the edge of the bed. "Wrap your legs around me."

Her legs slid around his muscle-thick waist and of a sudden his manhood was snugged against her sex, hard and slick, leaving no doubt he would fit—if it was the last thing she ever did.

He tightened his grip around her hips, and his gaze caught hers and held, refusing to release her as the tip of his shaft pressed against the entrance of her sex.

Masterful, that was the word that came to her.

Though this Rory was one she hardly knew, she trusted him.

She wanted him.

She had to have him.

She lifted onto one elbow as her other hand reached out. She needed to touch him. One by one, her fingers wrapped around his thick shaft. His eyes flared into black as the pupils pushed irises into thin turquoise rings. Her hand hardly fit around him as she gave a slow pull up his length. A groan poured from him, his gaze roving across her naked body, settling on her sex, open and aching to be filled by him.

"Like for like," he murmured.

"It's only fair."

Somehow as she stroked him, even as he pressed against her sex, her desire—nay, pure unadulterated *lust*—spiked higher.

"I need you," she said, her hips giving a restless swivel, desperate for even an inch of him.

His grip tightened around her, and he pushed forward. Her fingers released him as he entered her, inch by measured inch, her sex stretching to accommodate, oh, so much man.

"Should I stop?" he asked, flashing a bit of the Rory she knew.

She only realized she'd been biting her bottom lip between her teeth. "Don't you dare."

And there it was again: the glint of wickedness behind his eyes, and he continued his slow, deliberate penetration of her. A light sheen of perspiration pinpricked her skin. Oh, how much more of him could there possibly be?

He slid one arm behind her back, lifting as she continued to stretch around him, and gathered her close. "You control the motion."

Uncertainty flashed through her. She didn't like being uncertain. "I don't know how."

"Yes, you do."

The confidence in his gaze was enough for her. She wrapped her arms around his neck and crossed one ankle over the other behind him. It wasn't only her sex that felt so full of him, but her entire being to her soul.

He gave a shallow thrust, and she gasped. Instinctively, her hips swiveled against him, then they were moving with him, as he stroked in and out of her, oddly gentle. A strange sort of frustration clawed at her. "You're being too..." She trailed, squirming against him.

"Rough?" He sounded genuinely concerned.

"Polite," she corrected. "I shall not break. I can assure you."

"You're sure?"

She nodded. Whatever wickedness his body could devise for hers, she wanted.

The intention in his gaze doubled, and he took command of the pleasure doled out. Deeper he filled her, testing the limits of what she could tolerate. Oh, the exquisite pain and pleasure of coitus. How her body responded to it—this push and pull of boundaries she would only explore with him...pushing her even beyond them.

Her mouth found his neck and licked and sucked and nipped, spurring him on as the movement of his hips became more focused and unrelenting. Oh, what had she asked for?

This, a voice whispered.

The building sensation began winding through her sex again, turning her into a mindless entity. It was only her and this man and the pleasure they brought each other that mattered in the entire universe.

This feeling coiling and strumming through her sex was no easy mistress. It made demands on her. "Rory, oh, I don't know… I don't know…"

"Shh," he said. "You don't have to know, *here*." He touched her forehead. "You only have to *feel*"—he cupped a breast and angled his head to suck a hardened tip. She arced back as he moved in and out of her—"*me*."

She wasn't sure if it was his words or the caress of his slick tongue or the feel of his heavy cock—*oh, what a word*—but her entire being was suddenly concentrated *there*—her sex at his, joined, the slide of flesh across flesh.

Then that mechanism flipped in her mind, and it wasn't enough. Her hips increased their rhythm and his thrusts impaled her deeper and her breath caught in her lungs as she perched on the edge of a great height, oblivion suspended before her. All she wanted—*needed*—was to tip over that edge and give in to the void.

He thrust once…twice… And she tumbled over, but instead of falling, a part of her not bound by physical limitation took wing, as all that had gathered within burst in a flood of light and color and sensation, her sex pulsing its release around him in butterfly flutters.

The pleasure of *this*—it was almost too much. "You're almost too much," she whispered against his lips, unwilling to let go of the intimacy of their connection, even as his thrusts took on a relentlessness.

On a sudden groan, he pulled from her and wrapped sure fingers around his shaft. Transfixed, she watched him stroke his shaft, up and down its long, thick length. *Beautiful.* Then climax was pouring out of him on a shout, his seed spilling onto the sheets.

How could a single act be so of the body and yet so beyond those bounds, too? It was both the most physical experience of her life and the most elevated—a place where earth and heaven met and combined.

He reached for her. "Here."

She allowed him to settle her beneath the covers and rest her head on his shoulder. She was a woman of many words, and yet here, now, she found no need to speak them.

"You're composing poetry in your mind, aren't you?"

"Perhaps."

A lazy chuckle rumbled in his chest.

But it wasn't true.

The poetry had been writ already—his body onto hers, and hers onto his.

Words were rendered unnecessary.

It was the poetry their bodies understood—the only poetry that mattered.

ACROSS DARK, SILENT corridors Rory stepped, a sleeping Juliet in his arms. It was imperative she was returned to her bed before the household awakened. He would have no whispers bandied about her.

For she was his future bride.

Albeit convincing her was another matter entirely.

He could see a few obstacles in his path.

First, there was the matter of Miss Dalhousie. He was up a stump there. Juliet thought him madly, desperately in love with Miss Dalhousie, when nothing could be further from the truth.

It wasn't Miss Dalhousie he was madly, desperately in love with.

But it was the second obstacle that he saw as the more substantive one. Juliet had it in her head that she wouldn't marry.

Yet it occurred to him that he might have a weapon at hand.

Her desire.

For him.

He never would've thought he had anything to offer Miss Juliet Windermere. But now he saw that he did.

As improbable as that was.

He would convince Juliet to be his by means fair or foul.

The logic was simple.

She wanted him. He wanted her.

He felt no guilt about using her desire against her to get what they both wanted—each other.

Which was why he would continue the ruse that he was still interested in Miss Dalhousie.

To spend time with Juliet.

She was already head over heels in lust with him.

Now to convince her heart to follow her body.

Chapter Ten

Two days later

R ORY STOOD AT the front doorstep of Dalhousie Manor and tucked a skeleton key inside his trouser pocket. His informal visit to the kitchens had met with success.

But that was for later.

After his night with Juliet, he'd settled on a strategy.

Sometimes in the absence of a source of burning desire, one's desire increased.

So, he'd stayed away in the absurd hope that would give her a few thoughts.

Two days later, here *he* was—the one unable to stay away a day longer.

It called into question which of them his strategy had done its work upon.

He adjusted his cravat, only just resisting the impulse to sniff his armpits. He hadn't been this nervous at the prospect of seeing a lass since his green youth. He needed to be at his best. After all, he was here to convince a very strong-minded lass to be his.

Satisfied that all about him was in order and he didn't reek of farm toil, he lifted the door knocker and gave it three firm raps. A few seconds later, the door swung open, and Rivers appeared, his cheeks flushed and his eyes harried.

"Is all well, Rivers?" asked Rory, alarmed.

"All is as it's been these last seven or so days, milord," said the aged butler, standing aside to allow Rory entry.

Seven or so days.

Since the arrival of Juliet and Delilah.

"Ah," said Rory, handing Rivers his greatcoat, a garment necessary in Scotland—even in spring, depending on the mood of the day.

He crossed the entry corridor that opened into the receiving hall and found a room transformed. It was now a proper theater, with the stage and frame completely finished and twenty or so chairs arrayed before it for the audience. Greenery had been brought in and arranged about the room. Rory sensed Juliet's talented hand.

Speaking of Juliet…

She, along with Delilah, and the whole host of Dalhousie brothers were gathered about the stage area. No one noticed his presence at the back as everyone concentrated upon individual tasks—some engaged in painting a backdrop, others pacing about the boards rehearsing their lines.

But it was Juliet and Delilah who held his gaze as they faced one another in the center of the stage, looking suspiciously like combatants. Perhaps they were enacting a scene… But, no, Delilah looked decidedly put out with her cousin, while Juliet wore her customary cool, impossible-to-penetrate smile.

Rory had been the recipient of that smile more times than he could count. In fact, until very recently, he'd thought that was simply her smile. But now he knew it for what it was: a defense fortified by a will as strong as steel.

And Delilah knew it, hence her brow creased in utter frustration.

"The fact is, Delilah," said Juliet, "there is no harm in it."

"No harm in it?" huffed Delilah. "Those are Shakespeare's words." A beat. "*Shakespeare.*"

Clearly, Juliet was accustomed to passionate defenses from her cousin, for she continued, undeterred. "But it was Shakespeare who understood that language evolved. He himself evolved it on many occasions."

Delilah remained utterly unmoved by Juliet's argument.

Rory had no idea who would win the row, but it hardly mattered to him. He only had eyes for Juliet—her quiet boldness, her confidence, not to mention her beauty.

This bold, confident, beautiful woman had once held a secret infatuation for him.

And he hadn't noticed.

Well, he was noticing now, though he might need to have his sight tested and take up spectacles, for how hadn't he seen *her*?

"Greetings and salutations, Lord Kilmuir," Oliver Quincy called out from his self-appointed place of overseeing the painting of the backdrop. "Are you come to engage in our amateur theatrics?"

In unison, Juliet and Delilah's heads whipped around.

But it was one pair of eyes the clear, bright green of spring buds that caught his. Surprise shone in those depths. Curiosity, too. And something else…

Pique.

If he wasn't very much mistaken, Juliet was irritated.

With him.

The possibility existed that his plan of staying away for a few days might've been a bad one.

"And where have *you* been?" demanded Delilah. "It's been four days since you've shown your face for rehearsal."

Rory ripped his gaze away from Juliet when every instinct demanded he stride directly to her, toss her over his shoulder, and make right whatever had gone wrong with her. "What with all the rain and piglets and my dog—"

Juliet snapped to. "Clootie? What about her?"

"It was something she ate. She's herself again."

But Juliet didn't seem yet satisfied. "You're keeping an eye?"

"Aye," he reassured her. How could he not be half in love with a woman who harbored a soft spot for his shaggy beast of a dog?

"Have you even looked at your lines, Rory?" asked Delilah.

"I wasn't aware I had any," he said. "Wasn't I to be a carpenter?"

Delilah gave a tiny roar of frustration. "I suppose you can be Charles."

Rory shrugged. It made not an iota of difference to him.

"I thought *I* was to be Charles," piped up Quincy.

Delilah flicked an indifferent wrist. "You can be Hymen."

Quincy's chest puffed out. "The god of marriage suits me perfectly well. Am I to take a dual meaning from that bit of casting, Lady Delilah?" he asked, looking entirely too pleased with himself.

"Pardon?" Delilah looked utterly nonplussed.

"That perhaps you have marriage on your mind of late?" The man winked.

Delilah met Quincy's eye directly and held it. "No."

A throat cleared behind Rory. Ravensworth had chosen this moment to make his presence known.

Rory nodded in greeting for his old friend. "Sebastian."

"Rory," said Ravensworth before addressing the room at large, and Delilah in particular. "I see a problem with the casting of Charles."

"You would," muttered Delilah who had taken a sudden interest in her copy of the play.

"If I'm not mistaken," he continued, "Charles is the wrestler in *As You Like It*."

"Mm-hmm," was all he got from Delilah.

"Who is defeated by Orlando."

She tapped her copy of the play. "It's all here in black and white."

"And James Dalhousie is to play Orlando?"

James stepped away from the backdrop he'd been painting, brush still in hand. "I am."

Ravensworth pointed toward James. "So *he* is supposed to defeat *him*?" He was now pointing at Rory, who had a good six inches and three stone on the lad.

"It does rather defy belief," said Juliet, ever the voice of reason.

Except when she was begging for his touch.

Rory gave himself a mental shake. This wasn't the time or place.

Later.

Delilah's jaw clenched and unclenched. "It's a play. It's all about setting reality away from the world of the stage, isn't it?"

Of everyone, James remained unmoved. "I could take him anyway."

Rory realized the lad was talking about him. A mouthy lad, to be sure.

Ravensworth barked a hearty laugh. "I don't suggest putting it to the test any time soon, old boy."

A few chuckles sounded around the stage. James' fists clenched at his sides. The boy certainly felt the need to prove his mettle. Rory remembered that particular masculine feeling at his age.

Well, the lad would figure it out. Rory had more important matters on his mind—like Miss Juliet Windermere.

Right.

He found himself striding up the center aisle, stopping only when he reached the front of the stage. He held out his hand. "Miss Windermere, would you like to practice our lines together?"

Her straight black eyebrows lifted with surprise. But he could see no help for it. He needed to get her alone, and the direct seemed the only way.

She opened her mouth, but it was a flabbergasted Delilah who answered, "But Charles the Wrestler and Celia don't speak any lines together."

The statement of the obvious landed in the room like a solid object.

"Perhaps," began Juliet, her unflinching gaze fixed upon him, "you've left your copy of the play at Baile Ìm and would like to borrow my copy?"

"Erm, aye."

She took his hand and allowed him to help her descend. "My copy is in the small drawing room. I'll show you your lines."

And with that, Rory followed Juliet away from the chaos of a stage production in rehearsal, his gaze having a devil of a time being gentlemanly and staying elevated at her shoulders. The narrow valley where her shoulder blades met beckoned the eye down the long length of her spine to the subtle sway of her hips—and a little lower, well, that would be her sweet, round arse, wouldn't it?

Two days had been too long without this view.

A few right turns had them out of the receiving hall. Knowing the house as he did, Rory saw that Juliet was, indeed, leading him to the small drawing room.

He had other ideas.

On impulse, he reached out and caught her hand from behind. She cast a questioning glance over her shoulder. "What are you—"

He gave his head a silencing shake and twined his fingers through hers. "Come with me."

She looked as if she might resist, then she let him draw abreast with her. The question hadn't left her eye, but she hadn't pulled her hand away from his either. He liked the feel of her hand in his. Slender and elegant, like the rest of her.

But it was more than the humid press of her skin against his.

It was the trust given.

Down one corridor, then another, he led her, the silence between them easy. He liked that. But it also held a tension.

He might like that better.

Without tension, there couldn't be release.

Soon, they were walking through a disused wing of the manor, the only sound the muted fall of their footsteps across second-best, Aubusson rugs.

"We played hide-and-seek here as children," she observed on a laugh. "When you and Archie could be convinced to actually seek us."

"You remember." He wasn't sure her memory cast him in the most heroic light.

"I once stayed hidden in the darkest corner of a wardrobe for an entire hour before I realized no one was coming to find me."

"I hope you don't still hold it against me."

She gave a little shrug. "It was a good plan to rid yourselves of annoying little sisters for an afternoon."

"Perhaps not my best moment."

Her eyes sparked with mischief. "Perhaps you could make it up to me."

That spark of mischief sent a lightning bolt of desire zigzagging through him. "Perhaps."

Once they reached the door he sought, he stood aside and allowed her to enter first. For a room that saw guests perhaps twice a year, it was clean and bright, not a mote of dust floating on the air.

He closed the door and retrieved the skeleton key from his trouser pocket.

Juliet's brow lifted. "Is this a kidnapping?"

He inserted the key into the lock, but didn't twist. "I'll leave it to you to turn the lock, if that's what you choose."

A dark light flashed behind her eyes. *Desire.* The idea sent a responding feeling coursing through him. Perhaps, even now, her thighs were pressing together beneath her skirts…

Exactly how he wanted her.

"I always did like this little study," she said, glancing around.

Rory stepped to the bow window. "For its view overlooking the kitchen garden?"

Juliet smiled. "For exactly that reason. The kitchen is the beating heart of every estate."

"Most ladies prefer a window that sweeps out to a picturesque view."

"I'm not most ladies."

"Don't I know it?"

She might've blushed, but he couldn't be sure as she took a seat on the saffron damask chaise longue. He remained standing at the window, propping a shoulder against the frame.

Her head canted with curiosity. "How did you come by the key to this room?"

"Mrs. Rush."

"The housekeeper gave you the key?" she asked, incredulous.

"Well, I happen to know where she keeps the keys to all the rooms, and she finds the dimple in my left cheek charming." He shrugged.

"The one when you half smile."

"Aye." He gave her just the smile. "She won't notice the key has taken a walk for an hour or so."

Juliet worried her bottom lip between her teeth. "Is there a reason you've brought me to this particular study? You couldn't have known it was my favorite."

In fact, he'd brought her to this room for two reasons. It was in the least used wing of the manor and…

It had a comfortable chaise longue.

"Perhaps," she continued, "you brought me here because it's also Miss Dalhousie's favorite room and you thought it would provide me inspiration?"

Rory snorted. She was toying with him, surely. But he could see from the seriousness in her eyes that she wasn't.

"Erm, perhaps," was the best response he could give that wasn't an outright lie.

Juliet's gaze narrowed skeptically. "I've been writing the poem."

Ah, this was better. "And how is Scáthach faring today?"

Juliet shook her head. "Not that poem. The other one. The one for Miss Dalhousie."

Oh.

"The one I'm writing to woo her."

He shifted against the wall. "Of course."

"I took quite a bit of inspiration from the last place you showed me."

Rory's eyebrows gathered in a bunch. "The inside of my bedroom?"

A beat of time laden with the events that had transpired between them in his bedroom two nights ago loped past.

"The waterfall," she said, at last.

Of course.

"Which does bring me to a point of curiosity," she continued. "I've never seen Miss Dalhousie leave the indoors, except to take a carriage ride. She seems quite content to be within doors. All the time."

Rory had no interest in—or intention of—discussing Miss Dalhousie. It wasn't for that purpose that he'd brought Juliet to this room. But he couldn't very well tell her as much.

Not with his words, at least.

He shrugged off his morning coat and tossed it toward the nearest chair.

A little frown pulled at the corners of her mouth. Her eyes followed as he unbuttoned his dove-gray waistcoat. "What, precisely, are you doing?" she asked, a pettish note to the question.

He was digging beneath her skin.

Good.

"It's a bit close in here, don't you think?"

She drew herself fully upright, all prim cool. "Not at all."

"No?" He loosened his cravat and let it—and his shirt—fall open. "You look a trifle flushed yourself."

"Not at all."

The woman with every word in the English language at her command was repeating herself.

Another promising development.

An unconscious hand swiped across her neck and put the lie to her words.

She was flushed, indeed.

And he knew for fact what he'd only guessed at two nights ago.

She couldn't resist him.

Which left him with only one more thing to say…

"Are you going to turn the key in the lock?"

Chapter Eleven

"ARE YOU GOING *to turn the key in the lock?*"

Juliet should gasp in ladylike shock.

She should shoot to her feet and flee the licentiousness being proposed beneath the outer layer of that question.

What happened the other night was to have been but once.

Rory began rolling up one, then the other, sleeve of his shirt, exposing forearms sinewy with muscle and fuzzed with golden hair.

And she knew she wouldn't flee.

With that simple question, he'd brought her not only to the point of decision, but to the point of commitment. There would be no doubts of intention between them. For there he stood, languid, with his exposed chest and forearms and with that particular dark expression in his eyes, looking like Adonis, and who was she to resist?

After all, she was only a woman.

She rose to her feet and, with firm decision, walked to the door. Her heart a butterfly in her chest, she twisted the key in the lock. She turned and pressed her back against solid wood, not ready to move toward him yet. "This was a bold idea, you know. *Here*, at Dalhousie Manor, in full light of afternoon."

"Boldness wins the day."

"I take it neither of us is going to apologize for the other night."

"No."

She pushed off the door and took a step. The way he was propped against the wall…his shirt a wide V exposing the muscles of his chest…his arms crossed before him showing bare forearms to particular advantage…the cock of his head…the wickedness in his eyes…the knowing curve of his smile…the dimple in his left cheek…

They all added to one undeniable truth.

A man who looked like he wanted nothing more than to be ravished.

By her.

Again.

She took another step, drawn to him by a force she was powerless to control. "And here I thought your penchant for wickedness extended only to bedrooms."

He gave his head a slow shake. "My penchant for wickedness extends to rooms where I find myself alone with you."

His words poured through her like molten lava.

She stopped a mere foot away, their gazes locked. She reached out and caressed the side of his face, sharp cheekbones and soft beard beneath her fingertips. She saw in his eyes permission—to touch him…to make him hers for as long as they were alone in this room together.

She would make the most of it.

She pulled his shirt from his trousers and lifted it over his head. One advantage of being a tall woman, she supposed. Though, unlike many men, he had yet a few inches on her. The garment landed unnoticed on the floor.

Solid and bulky from farm labor, he was all gorgeous man in the bright daylight. Her fingers couldn't resist exploring the ridges and valleys of his sculpted torso before following the dusting of hair down to the waistband of his trousers. "Oh, Rory," she muttered. "Just look at you."

A chuckle rumbled through his chest.

She met his eyes, unable to match his humor, for she was utterly serious. "I need to see the rest of you."

Oh, and there was his wickedness twining alongside the humor in his eyes. "As you please, my lady."

And his mouth when he smiled like that… She needed to kiss it. She lifted onto the tips of her toes and pressed her lips to his, their breath mingling. It was a kiss that promised more…*later*.

First, she had more exploring to do.

And perhaps other parts of his body to kiss.

She tore her mouth from his and met his dark, wicked gaze. A dare glinted in there. The rigid bulge pressing against brown superfine drew her eye. Instinctively, her palm grazed along the hard length, pulling a rumble from him.

Until this very moment, she hadn't been certain what to do next. But now, feeling *him*, an idea began to form… She could do more than kiss him above his waistband.

She flicked open a few buttons and the fall of his trousers released and there *he* was—long, thick, hard…begging for a touch…begging for a lick.

As she lowered to her knees, driven by this novel feeling, he caught her beneath the chin, forcing her to meet his gaze. "Is this what you want?"

The answer was simple. "Yes."

And she continued her descent, one hand instinctively wrapping around his hip to find his taut bottom. She gave it a squeeze. *Hard*, like the rest of him. Fingertips feathered along the velvety length of his shaft, its pulse throbbing with promise. She breathed *him* in…salt…pine…the deep, complex scent of man…musk and earth and vital.

She lifted her gaze and met his eye and held as she dragged her tongue up his hot shaft. She hadn't any idea if she was going about this the correct way, but the flaring of his pupils, turning his eyes nearly black, told her she was doing something right. How intimate was the smooth, hard, searing feel of this skin against hers. In a strange way, the intimacy of the other night was nothing to this.

Her mouth parted, opening to accommodate his girth as she took him in. His hand found the top of her head, his fingers weaving through her hair and clutching. The room's only sound was the ragged in and out of his breath as her hand tightened around him and developed a rhythm with her mouth as he penetrated deeper.

Lightning borne of want and need—longing and lust— streaked through her veins, tore through her body, creating a void inside her that opened wider with every slide of his manhood inside her mouth...every flick of her tongue against him...every moan that poured from his parted lips...every uttered, "*Juliet.*"

Her name on his mouth while her lips were wrapped around his shaft...

This was wickedness.

This was intimacy.

This was all she ever wanted.

"*Juliet,*" he said again, but a change in his voice. "We must stop."

Without releasing him, she gave her head a little shake. They'd only gotten started.

He chuckled. "*You* must stop," rasped across his throat. "Or I won't be able to."

And she caught his meaning. He was nearing release.

Well, that wouldn't do.

Not yet, anyway.

Slowly, she pulled back, his length slipping from her mouth one inch at a time. Before he pulled completely away, she gave his manhood a parting kiss.

He slid his hands beneath her shoulders and lifted. As she stood before this man mostly naked in all his masculine beauty, she became acutely aware that she was still fully clothed.

Again, that word came to her. *Transgressive.*

And another one, too.

Delicious.

Dark intention in his eyes, he pulled her to him with one hand as his other reached beneath her skirts, trailing up her thighs. Then his fingers were sliding against the swollen flesh of her slit. "Just as I thought," he rumbled into her ear.

"What?" she exhaled, gasping at the slick friction of his calloused fingers against her.

"Wet."

Oh, that a single three-letter word could incite a riot of need inside her. But—*oh*—she needed—*oh*—*more* of him...*now*. She would burst into a ball of flame if she didn't have him. Her hips gave a greedy swivel, aching for more of his touch.

Of a sudden, he pressed his hand firmly against her lower back, hips now against hers, his cock hot and hard between their bodies, and stepped her backwards until her bottom bumped against a desk. She gave a short hop and perched onto the oak edge, still fully clothed, but her skirts gathered about her hips, the only flesh exposed her most intimate parts—the skin of her thighs above her garters and...her quim with its dusting of black curls and pink center. The ravenous look in his eyes as he feasted upon the view was nearly enough to bring her to the point of release.

But not yet...

She parted her knees wide and reached for him, giving herself utterly and completely over to wickedness, as her arms twined around his neck. He stepped between her legs, and she pulled his face to hers, greedy for every touch she could have of him. As her lips touched his, so, too, did his manhood graze against her slit.

A jagged groan poured from her. "I need you inside me," she spoke against his mouth. *"Now."*

Her tongue met his in a carnal tangle, her hips pressing forward, this sheer need overwhelming her. He reached between them and guided the head of his manhood to the entrance of her sex.

"Greedy for it, are you?"

"Oh, yes," she groaned, her legs wrapping around his waist.

But he didn't push into her in the rush she all but demanded. Inch by deliberate inch, he penetrated her, taking his time, letting her quim adjust to his girth. Sparks flew where they touched—her hands roving across the furred muscles of his chest and back…his fingers toying with her breasts, squeezing the hardened tips…the join of his cock inside her quim… even there—especially there—with every push in and out of her, as their coupling took on a demanding, unrelenting rhythm, the desk groaning beneath them. A sheen of perspiration pinpricked her skin. It could almost be described as animalistic, except…

It wasn't.

This joining of his body with hers was *more*.

He lowered his head to take one of her nipples into his mouth. Her head arced back when he lightly bit down and landed a direct hit of pleasure in the center of her sex. "Do…*oh*…do that again," she begged.

He sucked her other nipple into his mouth, his tongue teasing the tip.

The now-familiar coiling sensation began winding her sex tight, taking her in its grip, turning her into naught more than a frenzied vessel of need with every thrust. Again, his teeth nipped her tight bud, and without warning, her sex broke in sudden climax, pulsing its release around him.

"Juliet," he muttered against her. "You are a revelation."

Here was *more* as she lifted outside herself, her hands gripping his shoulders while he impaled her upon his turgid length—*relentless, focused*—his own pleasure driving him toward his own completion.

Her quim felt spent and like he was too much and yet it still wanted this.

This was the territory that extended beyond the carnal and animal and into the place that contained their souls.

With a muffled roar into the curve of her throat, his release collapsed onto him, and he spent his seed. In the aftermath of seconds slower than the usual beat of time, his movements eased, but he didn't part from her. Instead, he gathered her closer into the secure warmth of his embrace, his breath ragged against her shoulder.

"Rory," she muttered into his neck. "I never knew this about you."

"What is that?" He hadn't lifted his face from her hair.

"How magnificent you are."

"I am a rather large, lumbering fellow."

She angled her head without pulling fully away and caught his turquoise gaze. "Not your body. *You*, Rory. *You* are magnificent."

He tensed, and she had the distinct feeling she'd spoken precisely the wrong words.

"Ah."

He pulled away. She experienced loss the instant he separated from her.

How was it she was now only whole when he was inside her?

He tugged her skirts down over her knees, the fabric dropping to her shins.

"*Ah?*" She'd said something wrong, but couldn't understand what.

He buttoned the fall of his trousers, his chest still bare. "You are new to this."

"*This?*"

"Tupping."

Her brow lifted as she waited in silence for him to continue.

"You're not yet acquainted with the particular feelings that flow through the body and mind after a good—"

"*Tup?*" She was, however, familiar with the particular feeling that was currently flowing through her. *Pique.* "Would you care to explain it to me?"

He spread his hands wide. "It's just that sometimes it provokes people to express emotions that they likely won't feel as strongly in an hour or so."

She nodded slowly. "So, you're saying that in sixty minutes I won't find you quite as magnificent as I do now?"

"I might've sunk to middling by then." He hesitated. "Or worse."

"*Or worse?*"

Darkness flashed behind his eyes. "You might think me a rake by then," he said, low and sincere.

"I'll never think that about you, Rory." It was only the truth. Besides… "Perhaps I'm the rake."

"Can a lady be a rake?"

"Perhaps." She considered the question. "It depends on how the power is balanced between the two people."

"And how is the power balanced between us?"

A good question.

One she wasn't prepared to answer.

It was this desire that kept spiking through her. She wanted him again. His mouth upon her. Hers upon him. Their sexes joined. The intimacy of that union.

She wanted to test the balance of power between them with their bodies.

He slid his shirt over his head and made quick work of dressing. She took the opportunity to straighten the twist of her bodice and reassemble her hair into a knot at her neck.

"Will you be attending the village assembly tomorrow evening?" he asked.

"I've promised Delilah. She would like to invite the village to our performance."

"And how do Mr. and Mrs. Dalhousie feel about that?"

"They are completely under her spell."

He smiled, but it didn't quite reach his eyes. He glanced toward the locked door. "Will you leave first? Or shall I?"

Juliet didn't hesitate. "You." She needed a moment to gather herself.

Rory looked as if he would say more. Instead, he closed the distance between them, tucked his thumb beneath her chin, and tipped her head back. His mouth grazed across her lips for a bright instant of contact, then was gone.

When she opened her eyes, the door was closing behind him.

Somehow, alongside the carnality and wickedness that blazed between them could exist *this*…a sweet parting kiss.

Rory…wicked and sweet—a combination of ingredients only recently discovered.

And yet she was ravenous and insatiable for them.

She'd always possessed a sweet tooth.

And yet…was he her sweet to sample?

Wasn't he, in fact, destined to be Miss Dalhousie's?

The thought unleashed a definite and resounding *no* inside her, as every cell in her body rejected the idea.

It was only now—now that the haze of lust was fading—that she was able to string together a few rational thoughts. One of which was quite plain and simple:

She'd taken matters too far with Rory.

Her heart was going to break when this was all over. A sliver of a crack might've already formed.

There was only one thing for it.

She must finish the poem.

And finish whatever madness that had sprung between her and that magnificent, sweet, secretly wicked man.

Chapter Twelve

Next evening

A THRILL OF anticipation shimmered through Juliet as she sat before the dressing table mirror securing the blush-pink flower crown. Spring blossoms in their hair had been Delilah's idea.

How Juliet loved a village assembly. One could relax the rules and enjoy a bit of fun, without concern that one was talking to the *wrong sort*. The village assembly diluted matters of class for a few hours as everyone happily mingled together—a far superior experience to any ball offered in London.

Delilah leaned over her back and rested her chin on Juliet's shoulder. A shallow worry line had settled between Delilah's eyebrows this last week. Juliet reached up and squeezed her cousin's hand. "You know the play will be wonderful."

The worry line deepened. "I don't know that at all."

"I do."

A rueful smile ticked about Delilah's mouth. "The Orlando to my Rosalind is several years younger than I and half a head shorter."

"In all fairness, we Windermere lasses are a tall lot, and with those lanky limbs of his, James Dalhousie does show promise to be a towering, strapping man someday."

Delilah snorted. "Unless he can achieve that stature in the next twenty-four hours, it's of no use to me."

The cousins' eyes met in the mirror, and giggles couldn't help bubbling up. "I have a feeling I'll need to accustom myself to the sound of laughter before opening night," said Delilah.

"It'll be a smashing success," said Juliet, giving her cousin's hand a reassuring squeeze.

"And Scáthach?" asked Delilah. "Are you finding inspiration for her poem?"

"Somewhat," said Juliet, releasing Delilah's hand. Her gaze shifted. She had no intention of revealing that her latest source of inspiration came in the form of one very large, auburn-haired Scotsman.

Delilah straightened and took a step back, head canted subtly to the side. "With Archie and Amelia married off, it's just the two of us."

Juliet swiveled around on her seat so she could meet Delilah's gaze directly. "It's really only ever been the two of us."

"But for how much longer, I wonder."

The moment grew heavy with an unexpected seriousness. "Surely, you're not thinking of accepting Oliver Quincy," said Juliet, seeking to lighten the mood.

That got a dry laugh out of Delilah. "Hardly," she said, but it hadn't been enough to distract her. "Juliet, since our arrival in Scotland, you seem a bit—" Her eyes screwed up to the ceiling as she searched for the correct word. "Altered."

"Oh?" Juliet gave a breezy one-shouldered shrug. "I am very much my same self, I can assure you."

Delilah looked decidedly unconvinced. "Are you?" Her head canted to the other side. "Really, since the night you were stranded at Rory's."

Juliet resisted the sudden need to swallow. Delilah would catch it. "I can't imagine why that would be."

A lie, of course.

She could imagine.

And did.

Vividly.

Especially at night.

In bed.

A *hmm* loaded with meaning sounded from Delilah.

Juliet knew she must change the subject, or Delilah wouldn't stop until she had the truth pouring from Juliet's mouth.

Rory was the only secret she'd ever kept from Delilah—first as an infatuation, now as a lover.

And the poem for Miss Dalhousie… It lay hot and flat against her skin beneath the silk of her stays.

That was a secret, too.

She'd worked on it all through last night until it was complete, not finding her bed until dawn. But it was done. That was the point.

And soon she and Rory would be done, too.

She would be giving it to him tonight.

Delilah opened her mouth, surely to apply additional pressure, for she could be relentless when she sensed a secret. Juliet knew exactly how to head Delilah off. "I've noticed," said Juliet, "you can be a bit altered yourself."

Delilah's brow lifted. "Oh?"

"When Ravensworth enters a room."

Instantly, all the mischief fled Delilah's face, and anger flashed behind her eyes for the split of a second, replaced the next instant by an uncharacteristic layer of hardness. "You're usually so sensible, cousin," she said, distant and utterly unlike herself, "but what rot you're speaking now. You can complete your toilette without me, I'm sure."

With that, Delilah pivoted on one heel and left Juliet alone in the room. She'd scraped a raw nerve within Delilah, but she couldn't regret it. In fact, she felt relief as to have so thoroughly distracted her cousin.

Juliet couldn't talk about Rory.

Or how he altered her.

Her hand brushed across her bodice and the poem there.

A poem to help Rory woo another woman.

And she only had herself to blame for it.

But before that, she had a village assembly to attend where she intended to dance her slippers off and forget her troubles for a few hours.

Wasn't that what dances were for, anyway?

Two hours later

JULIET STILL FULLY intended to dance her slippers off at some point in the evening, but first, she needed to break free from Oliver Quincy, who was presently talking the ears off her and any other unfortunate person who happened to amble within listening distance.

And to make matters worse, Delilah—contrarian to the last—had decided to fully engage with the pompous nodcock. "Why take issue with a traveling Shakespeare company in the area?" asked Delilah.

Quincy exhaled a long-suffering sigh, his mouth curving in the supercilious smile he'd perfected as his particular artform. One could almost admire it, from afar…from very afar.

"A traveling troupe of *actors*"—Quincy uttered the word with particular disdain, and without consideration that the lady he'd been attempting to court these last three years was, in fact, an actress—"is little better than a band of gypsies. Horses and all manner of farm implements will have gone missing by morning. Mark my words."

A few of the assembled had gathered around and were nodding in assent. Not Delilah. Her cheeks and eyes contained the bright, sharp glint of irritation held at bay. "The tradition of the traveling theater company is a centuries-old practice," she said, reasonably. Too reasonably. Juliet didn't trust Delilah when she was being too reasonable. "It's as noble a trade as any. Nobler, in fact."

"Nobler?" Quincy scoffed and shook his head in mild forbearance. "While it is somewhat charming that you enjoy dabbling in theatrical pursuits, Lady Delilah, how do you figure that?" He gave a corrective shake of the head. "These ideas of yours. A husband could help guide you toward more ladylike modes of thought."

Delilah's fists clenched at her sides. If they'd still been in the nursery, Delilah would've already walloped Quincy over the head. And though they'd been out of the nursery for decades, and were ostensibly more civilized, Juliet wasn't sure a good walloping was too far removed from the realm of possibility.

Delilah kept her head and unclenched her fists. Juliet could breathe again.

"'Tis nobler," continued Delilah, "because a traveling theater company offers anyone with a coin in their pocket—from king to costermonger—a respite from the drudgery and responsibilities of everyday life. To spend an evening with the poetry of Shakespeare… What more could anyone want?"

Familiar movement caught the edge of Juliet's eye. She knew before her gaze shifted who she would find.

At the wide entrance to the main assembly room stood Rory and Ravensworth looking almost too splendid to gaze upon directly, dressed in their finest evening blacks. They wouldn't have been out of place at a London ball. Here, they certainly stood out, but she suspected that was rather the point. Not to lord it over the local village, but rather as a show of respect. If a duke and a viscount arrived at the assembly looking less than their impeccable best, the villagers might feel slighted, as if they weren't deemed worthy of the finest from a pair of eligible lords.

But, oh, how eligible they looked. Just by arriving, they'd suddenly become the sun around which this entire affair revolved. Juliet found herself, subtly stepping back. She would eventually hit wall, where she could observe their effect on the room.

But it wasn't to be.

Rory's eye caught hers, and he started walking…

Toward her.

As if she were somehow lodestone to his magnet.

How the idea appealed to her.

As if the pull of her left him no choice but to be here.

It was only after the two men joined their small grouping that Quincy acknowledged—or even noticed, more like—their presence. He gave them each a passing nod of acknowledgment and continued with his education of Delilah. "But, Lady Delilah, here is where your feminine brain has lost its way. Shakespeare's plays were performed by men and lads during his day. His work was never intended to be open to the interpretation of the fairer sex." He shrugged, as if helpless to the facts. "Surely, 'tis best to leave matters your mind couldn't possibly comprehend to the men. In this way, the balance between the sexes is maintained. Truly, all you need is a firm and dedicated husband to take you in hand, and you'll find yourself all the happier for it."

Juliet's mouth might've gaped fully open before she picked it up off the floor. She considered placing a restraining hand on Delilah's upper arm before she went for Quincy's throat. But Delilah simply stared at the man as if he'd suddenly sprouted another head, utterly befuddled.

Juliet darted a glance toward Ravensworth and Rory, who were watching the proceedings with no small amount of amusement. In fact, Ravensworth snorted. "A firm hand you say, Quincy?"

"Indeed."

"To bend her over one's knee and deliver a firm smack on the bottom, perhaps?"

Quincy nodded, judiciously. "As would be her husband's right."

Juliet's hand jumped to her mouth.

"In the interest of education?" asked Ravensworth, utterly committed to the absurdity.

"Of course."

Juliet's gaze shifted and found Rory's eye. He lifted a single eyebrow. A sudden giggle rose up, and she was powerless against it. Rory's face lit up in a smile, and he gave a loud guffaw. Juliet found Delilah observing her as if she'd committed a grave betrayal. Still, Delilah must've seen the humor in the exchange.

Perhaps not the part about the Duke of Ravensworth delivering a firm smack to her bottom.

Juliet coughed and cleared her throat. "Must've been something I ate."

"That gave you a laughing fit?" asked Quincy, observing her as if she were the silliest woman alive and was, in fact, making his case for him that women were brainless creatures.

As galling as that was, Juliet had no intention of disabusing him of the notion. "It happens on occasion."

She couldn't allow herself to meet Rory's gaze again.

They could now communicate without words.

That was new.

She didn't dislike it.

The string quartet who had been brought in all the way from Edinburgh—apparently Ravensworth's generous gift to the village tonight—chose that moment to strike up a waltz. A frisson of excitement sizzled through the air.

At the very same moment, Ravensworth and Quincy took a step forward, each holding out a white-gloved hand, and opened their mouths to say, "Lady Delilah, if you—"

But it was Quincy alone who finished the question. "Will do me the honor of this dance?"

Ravensworth's mouth snapped shut, looking as if he'd just bitten into an apple and found half a worm.

Delilah glanced back and forth between the two men, a mean, little smile playing about her mouth. "With each of you being men of such important distinction, how could I possibly choose between you?"

Ravensworth's face looked like thunder. Quincy, well, he remained utterly like Quincy. In fact, his chest might've puffed out.

Delilah tapped a contemplative finger to her mouth before stabbing it into the air. "Oh, I have the very answer."

Ravensworth had the good sense to look wary. Quincy, possessing not a lick of good sense to begin with, didn't. A note of hope hung about him. Juliet could almost feel pity for him…if it weren't for the fact that he was utterly unpitiable.

"Since you both wish to dance so badly, perhaps you could dance with one another."

And with that, Delilah whirled around—she'd ever been fond of a dramatic exit—and marched toward the ladies' retiring room.

Ravensworth pivoted and strode away in the opposite direction. Quincy gave his cravat a slight adjustment and made his way toward a group of men who had been particularly vocal about Parliament's recent passage of the Cruel Treatment of Cattle Act and how it would affect farmers.

Juliet found herself alone with Rory.

She shifted on her feet, suddenly unsure where to set her gaze. The tops of her slippers seemed the most logical place.

He cleared his throat, forcing her gaze to lift. "Would you do me the honor of this dance, Miss Windermere?" He held out his hand.

Juliet understood two facts at once.

She couldn't refuse him. Not after Delilah's little performance. Too many eyes were upon her and making assumptions—likely correct ones.

But even more… She didn't want to refuse him.

She wanted him to take her into his arms and sweep her across gleaming Scottish pine and not stop until the slippers had been danced off her feet.

She placed her hand in his. Through silk gloves his masculine warmth slid into her.

She'd never given much thought to the idea of feeling safe in a man's arms. In truth—and admittedly ungenerous to her own sex—she'd always half-thought the notion silly feminine fiddle-faddle. But when Rory led her the few feet to the dancing floor and placed his other hand on the indent of her waist, she felt secure and sure, like nothing beyond the circle of his arms could touch her.

He pulled her into the swirl of the waltz already begun, and her heart beat in rhythm to the light movements of her feet. Dancing was as close to flying as she would ever come. Her gaze lifted, and she found him staring down at her, lopsided smile tipping at his mouth. "You love to dance, Miss Windermere."

"I do, Lord Kilmuir."

"How is it we've never danced before now?"

"Simple," she said. "You never asked."

A line formed between his eyebrows. "Come to think of it, I don't recall seeing you at any dances."

"I was there. But you wouldn't have noticed me."

"Why is that?"

She laughed, the buoyant sound chorusing gaily with the laughter from the other waltzing couples. "Because I have a particular ability to blend into a wall when I so choose."

"No longer," he rumbled, a smile on his mouth, a seriousness in his eyes. He gathered her closer than was strictly proper and bent his head so his lips touched her ear. "You'll never be invisible to me, Juliet."

How his words, hot and humid against her skin, blazed an arrow of longing straight through her, to places only he had ever touched—in her body…in her soul.

She was helpless against such words.

She'd been infatuated with this man for nigh on a decade, but she understood now those had been a girl's feelings that only saw surfaces. This last week, she'd seen so much more of the man below his appealing surface. What she felt now ran deeper.

These feelings were a woman's.

"You'll never be invisible to me, Juliet."

Until this very moment, she'd been utterly unaware they were words she needed to hear.

They were as fresh droplets of rain upon parched earth.

Chapter Thirteen

Juliet released a sigh against Rory's neck, sending goose bumps cascading down his spine.

It was hard to escape the feeling that he was running out of time with her.

And it wasn't through his body that he would achieve his desired end.

He needed the words.

But for now he had the dance as they moved in step, the music of the strings a bright accompaniment to the music in his heart.

He had Miss Juliet Windermere in his arms.

He had Miss Juliet Windermere sighing into his neck.

He had Miss Juliet Windermere gazing up at him with those eyes the clear green of emeralds as if he were the only man on Earth.

As if she were the only woman for him.

"You are magnificent."

Those had been her words to him yesterday.

No one had ever said anything like that to him—or likely, believed it of him—not even himself.

Not until Juliet.

She believed him capable…*magnificent.*

And if she could believe it of him, he could be it.

It struck him that from the beginning they'd gone about the business of coming to know one another backwards. He knew the feel of every line and curve of her body. He knew precisely where to touch her—where to *lick* her…where to *nibble* her—to send her pupils flaring and legs trembling with naked desire. He knew how to bring her to the edge of release and tumble with her over it.

But he hadn't known *this*. How she felt in his arms as she moved with the music of a waltz.

To touch her in this formal way, open to the eyes of an entire village, was new.

"There is so much I don't know about you, Miss Windermere," he found himself saying, a mild panic striking through him.

A secret smile lit about her mouth. "But so much you do."

The music was winding to an end, and a sense of urgency took Rory over. Soon—within seconds—he would no longer have an excuse to touch her.

And that wouldn't do.

"Come with me," he said. He hoped he didn't sound as desperate as he felt.

"Where?"

"There's a place I want to show you."

A hard light passed behind her eyes. "Is it a place Miss Dalhousie—"

He wasn't about to let her finish the question. "A place *you* will love."

The stubborn set of her jaw was at odds with the battle in her eyes, as if her mind were telling her to refuse him, but her curiosity wasn't allowing her.

He searched for the correct combination of words, and of a sudden, he knew exactly what they were. "Another place we can dance."

A heartbeat later, she nodded. Curiosity had won the day.

He had won the day.

The waltz chose that moment to end with a sweeping flourish of strings. Rory held onto Juliet's hand as he rushed her off the dancing floor before anyone could take note and through the doors that opened onto the terrace. Their fingers twined, they stepped onto a path that led through a small stand of oaks. In silence and trust, she followed as they cleared the woods and began a short ascent up a rocky sheep scramble, their only light that of a gibbous moon and winking stars in the crystalline sky.

They came to halt at the top, the vastness of the nightscape all around them. "What am I looking at?" she asked, her voice thick with awe.

"Our fairy glen."

A narrow valley spread below them with grass that shone green muted with the slate-gray of night, stones of all shapes and sizes strewn about. All one had to do was look a little closer to see the rocks weren't scattered about, but precisely arranged into the shape of a large spiral.

"This place is magical," she whispered, as if not to disturb the magic.

"Aye."

Her gaze flicked toward him. "I do love it."

For an instant, his heart caught in his chest. *I...do...love...* A wild hope had surged that the sentence would end with a word different from *it*.

He gave himself a mental shake. He couldn't think of that other word.

Not yet, at least.

If ever.

He cleared his throat. "There's a fairy glen on the Isle of Skye, too."

"Oh?"

"It's considerably larger and more intricate."

She nodded with understanding. "A place Scáthach might've known."

"Aye."

She turned so she faced him squarely. "Didn't you lure me out here with the promise of a dance?"

"That I did, lass."

He reached for her hand and slipped her elegant fingers through his considerably thicker ones. Then he caught her at the small of her waist and pulled, her body swaying forward until she was fast against him, slender and soft against his bulkier form. Their feet began moving, not in the steps of a waltz or a mazurka or any other dance that might be happening in the assembly rooms at this very moment.

But in a dance of their own making.

This dance was simply them beneath the stars, moving to the beat of their hearts...the only music the in and out of their breath...the faint susurration of a summer night's breeze...the distant song of a nightingale.

Informal and intimate was this dance. No eyes upon them. Their eyes only for each other.

There were the intimacies of the body, and there was this— an intimacy that tapped a deeper well.

The intimacy he'd been seeking all along.

He'd sensed it thrumming beneath the other intimacies they'd shared, but hadn't known how to unlock it.

Their moonlit dance finished, he released the small of her back, but held on to her hand, and led them to a grassy patch of turf at the edge of the hill. He shrugged off his evening coat and spread it flat, wide enough for both of them. He took a seat, hoping she would follow his lead.

She did.

Together, they sat in silence, shoulder to shoulder, and gazed upon the fairy glen below, the inky, twinkling sky meeting the horizon on the far side of the valley.

He'd bound this woman to him with his body, but that wasn't enough.

It never had been.

He wanted her to be his.

Not for mere reasons of the body.

But for one deeper.

That of the heart.

"Not that I agree with Oliver Quincy very often," he began.

Juliet's head craned around to give him the full force of a horrified stare. Not the most auspicious beginning.

"Let us hope not," she gasped.

Rory forged on. He had something to say. "Still, Quincy may have made an important point in all his chatter, before, of course, missing the point entirely."

Juliet snorted. "As he is wont to do." She playfully nudged his shoulder with hers. "You've got my curiosity fully aroused."

What a choice of words. Here he was trying to form an intimacy deeper than the physical, and here was his physical—his *aroused* cock, namely—thinking of something deeper it could do.

"What important point did Oliver Quincy nearly make?" she asked.

"One about women."

"Doubtful," she said with absolute, dismissive finality.

"And men," continued Rory.

He was making a hash of this attempt at deeper intimacy. Perhaps he should just kiss her. Perhaps it was simply that he was better at convincing bodies to be his than at convincing hearts and souls.

"And what insight does Oliver Quincy *almost* have about women and men?"

"That women need protection."

Finally, he'd veered back on course.

Juliet scoffed. "I realize that I shall sound like the most spoiled lady in all the world when I say this, but I have never once in my life felt like I needed protection. Such is the privilege of my rank, wealth, and family situation."

Family situation. Something about that phrasing struck Rory.

But he couldn't let his point rest yet. "Not even from a man like—"

Her eyebrows crinkled together. "I hope you're not considering finishing that sentence with the name Oliver Quincy."

"*Me.*"

"*You?*" she asked. Her eyebrows released and shot toward the night sky.

"It does occur to me, yes."

"I could never want or need protection from you."

The way she spoke those words with such earnestness and sincerity sent a feeling skittering through him. Yet...

Family situation. He now understood why the phrase stuck. "Your parents would've protected you."

She blinked, and the moment transformed. Gone was the disdain and humor, and in its stead was sincerity and openness. He stepped into that opening. "Do you ever miss them?"

She set her gaze upon the fairy glen, head tilted, pensive. "It's not them, precisely, that I miss. I never knew my parents. Rather I have these ideas of them."

He reclined back onto his elbows, hoping the relaxed position would invite more confidences. "How so?"

"After they perished in the carriage accident, I came to live with my aunt, uncle, and cousins when I was barely toddling on two legs. My first strong memories aren't of my mother, but of Delilah." A wistful smile softened about her mouth. "She and I never left one another's sight for at least ten years. But I do have other early memories—faint ones—like memories that are echoes of other memories. I have a memory of my mother smiling at me, but I also have a portrait of her smiling and it's the same smile, so I don't know if the smile I recall was one given to me or a trick of my mind."

Rory didn't hesitate. "It's her smiling at you that you remember, Juliet. I'm sure of it."

He wasn't certain who needed it to be so more—her or him. He didn't like to see the supremely confident Juliet Windermere doubt herself.

"In some ways," she continued, "I'm very much like my Windermere cousins. But in others, I'm not. And, sometimes, I'll find myself wondering if the ways I'm *un*like them are the ways I'm like Mama and Papa. I'll never know."

The words Juliet was speaking to him were words she'd never told another living soul, he sensed. They were feelings that lived in her heart.

That she'd voiced them to him was a gift—one he wasn't about to take lightly.

She didn't think she needed a man to protect her in the world—and maybe she was right.

But he did know what sort of man she *did* need.

One to confide in.

One to hear the secrets of her heart.

One who would protect those.

And she had that man.

Him.

On instinct, he reached out and caressed the side of her face, his fingers sliding around to the nape of her neck. He tugged her toward him, and she swayed with the movement. Only a brief instant of hesitation—nay, *recognition*—and her lips were touching his and a now-familiar spark lit through him. The sort of spark that turned into a full conflagration when he deepened the kiss. It was all the physical sensation of the kiss—the feel of her soft mouth…the sweet taste of her…her specific heat—but it was more than the physical as she moved forward and needed him to steady her so she didn't tumble over him.

But that was just it. Her naked wanting. She didn't try to suppress or mask her desire. This honesty was impossible to resist. He would give her what she wanted every time she asked for it.

A feeling of possession streaked through him.

The gift of her was for him only.

Her mouth on his, her fingers found his cravat and made short work of the knot. Then her hands were beneath his shirt, roving across his chest. He gave in to the pleasure of being caressed by her as she gave in to the pleasure of caressing him. She liked all his muscles.

Clearly bent on ravishing him here and now, her hands trailed lower, and anticipation coiled inside him. If he wasn't very mistaken, she was about to… Her fingers grazed across the front of his trousers, across his hard cock that was full to bursting, pulling a long, animal groan from him.

She smiled against his mouth and increased the pressure, rubbing up and down his length. "Juliet," he rumbled.

"I like it when you say my name like that," she spoke into the intimate space between their mouths.

"Like a man on the brink of perishing from desire?"

"Yes."

That *yes* said so much more than *yes*. "Shall I pull my name from you in the way I like?"

Her pupils flared. "Please," she implored.

She liked it when he was wicked with her. From the look in her eyes, he already knew her sweet cunny was wet and throbbing and aching for his touch.

In a smooth, efficient motion he secured her by the waist and flipped them around so she was lying flat on his jacket, back supported by springy green turf. He removed one of her gloves, then the other, before taking one of her wrists, then the other, in one hand. "Do you trust me?"

Alongside the desire in her clear emerald gaze twined that other emotion.

Trust.

"Yes."

Chapter Fourteen

HIS.

The word anchored in Rory's mind as he stretched Juliet's arms over her head, her body vulnerable beneath him, and angled his head to kiss the curve of her neck…

Trailing his tongue along the line of her clavicle, down the décolletage of her breasts, her nipples taut and straining against the silk of her gown before his mouth ever reached them. With his other hand, he tugged at her bodice, exposing her chemise. He tugged again, baring her nipples to the night air and sucked, taking one into his mouth like the sweetest cherry. Her back arched, pushing her into him, her lips parted and a soft sigh released to the crisp night air.

Lower went his free hand, which began tugging at her skirts, pulling them up, up, up until silk and muslin hems bunched at her waist. He shifted to take in the view of her—the beauty of earth below and sky above nothing to the beauty of her—long, stockinged legs…twin patches of bare thighs leading to the dark curls of her sex…her eyes half-lidded with desire…her kiss-crushed lips parted and releasing sighs and moans of want and need.

She needed him to touch her…*there*.

Light fingertips brushed across her creamy thighs. One moment she was squeezing them together, the next she was splaying them apart. She'd gone mindless with desire.

He tightened the hand around her wrists as the other found her mons pubis, his rough fingertips grazing along her slit, wet and swollen from desire, as he'd known it would be. Her hips angled, pushing her against him, begging for more. He smiled and kept his touch feather light, eliciting a moan of frustration from her. When he decided she'd anticipated long enough, his finger trailed to the entrance of her sex. Her breath caught as he slowly pushed inside. *Tight. Wet.*

"Oh, yes," poured from the back of her throat, her eyes squeezed shut, her body a vessel of need.

A need he'd created.

A need only he could satisfy.

His.

His gaze fast upon her, she received the pleasure he gave and demanded yet more in return. "Greedy," he rasped into her ear.

Another finger joined the first, stretching her, filling her, pulling more moans from her, making her wild beneath his hand. When his cock could take no more, he withdrew from her, leaving her teetering on the edge of release, no doubt. Her eyes flew open, both questioning and slightly outraged, demanding he finish what he'd started.

Then he had the fall of his trousers open and his cock free and pressing at her entrance. In one swift, satisfying thrust of his hips, he was inside her. He went still, letting her adjust to him, yes, but also soaking her into his senses. Her slick heat around him. Her breath rasping humid against his neck. Her crisp scent of sage and jasmine mixed with the heady sex scent of woman.

Her hips swiveled, and his cock throbbed. She arched into him, demanding the release promised. He began moving his hips, sliding in and out of her, and her quim picked up where his fingers had left it—on the brink of climax.

"Juliet, you're going to release for me..." He licked his thumb and slipped it between their bodies, down to her sex, where her most sensitive flesh had only awaited his touch. *"Now."*

He slid his thumb against the hooded nub—her breath caught. He applied pressure and rubbed—she tensed and bit her plump bottom lip, a woman held entirely in his thrall. Another slick stroke—her back arched, eyes squeezed shut, the entirety of her being concentrated on the patch of skin where he touched her—then another…and she broke on a cry and pulsed her climax around his cock. "Rory," she gasped against his neck.

"And that's how I like you to say my name," he rumbled into her ear.

A languid smile replete with satiety curved about her mouth. He released her arms, which would start to ache if he continued to hold them above her head, but he stayed inside her, his mouth still pressed to her ear. "Now we have the first one out of the way."

"First?" she gasped. No small amount of awe in that gasp. "It can happen again?"

"Oh, aye, lass, and it will."

Her pupils flared at the promise.

She fully intended to hold him to it.

He began to move inside her again, to penetrate her with measured calculation and purpose. His own desire began to transform. This was need, raw and urgent, heightened by an emotion coursing through him that he'd never experienced.

This wasn't merely the coupling of two bodies.

It was the coupling of two souls…

Of two hearts.

And perhaps, she felt it, too.

This sense of oneness couldn't be all him.

It took two halves to make this whole.

Her legs wrapped around his waist, insisting he penetrate her deeper…*fully*. He slid a hand beneath her bottom, tilting her hips so she could receive more of him, and gathered her close, giving her what she wanted with sure, deliberate strokes, burying himself inside her to the hilt.

She gasped. "That feeling—*oh*—it's starting—*oh*—again."

And with those words, his shaft buried deep inside her, taking all he gave, she brought him to the edge with her. Sweat slicked his body as he thrust with intention, relentless, determined she would find release with him. Her head arched back, digging into green grass and exposing the elegant column of her throat, as she surrendered to mindless abandon. Control began to slip away as his rhythm increased and he lost himself inside her.

"*Rory*," she cried into his neck for the second time tonight.

As her quim pulsed around him, he gave in to the animal instinct to pump his release into her on a shout, joining her in the vastness of climax as deep and unknowable as the inky sky above. "Juliet, my love," he murmured as he collapsed to the side of her.

It was only when he began to return to himself that he realized what he'd said.

There wasn't a syllable he would take back.

When he pulled his face from her neck, it was to find her watching him, a question in her eyes. "You are quite an expert at lovemaking," she said. "Empirically speaking, of course."

A lazy chuckle rumbled in his chest.

As funny as she was intelligent. How many people knew that about Miss Juliet Windermere?

He did.

That was all that mattered.

"Aye," he said in answer to her observation.

He knew this about himself. He cared for the pleasure of his partner, unlike most men, apparently. He'd been told so on more than one occasion.

She went utterly serious. "You're more than that, you know."

"More than what?" Was he was missing something?

"You're more than your ability to deliver an excellent tup."

His laugh this time took on a note of discomfort.

"And those words you spoke?" she asked.

"Which ones?"

"Near the end."

Juliet, my love.

Those words, neither needed to say.

"Aye?"

"Were they simply words spoken in the heat of lovemaking?" she asked, direct. "Words that won't be felt as strongly in an hour or so?"

She was tossing his words from yesterday back at him.

Good.

He'd spoken them to provoke a response from her, and here it was, at last.

The time had arrived to give them a good airing out—and one word in particular.

He rolled off her completely. "I think we should be sitting upright—and bits tucked away—for this conversation," he said, doing precisely that as he folded himself into his trousers and buttoned the fall.

She sat up, tucking her breasts into her bodice. "I think you're right." She'd begun securing her flower crown.

What was it about a woman messing about with her hair that was so transfixing to a man?

He pushed to a stand and held out a hand for her. She grabbed hold, and he had her on her feet the next instant. Their hands held onto each other for a heartbeat of time, long enough for them both to notice. Neither wanted to break the contact, but each understood they must. He released her, and she retreated to a nearby outcropping of rock, balancing her hip against it for support.

He found his own boulder and waited. Juliet had something to say to him. Which was as well. He had something to say to her.

"Miss Dalhousie returns tomorrow for the performance."

"Oh?" Rory could groan with frustration. In truth, he'd forgotten about the woman's return. It didn't concern him. Nothing about Miss Dalhousie did, or ever would. But…

The woman before him didn't know that.

Right.

He'd made a right hash of matters, and that was a fact.

The time had arrived to fix them.

"I don't care that Miss Dalhousie is returning," he said. "I've never cared."

Juliet's eyebrows formed a straight line. "Never cared?"

"Not in a few years, at least."

"A few *years*?" With every word she spoke, the famously cool, calm, and collected Miss Juliet Windermere became increasingly agitated.

"Further," he continued. If she didn't like what he'd already said, she certainly wouldn't like this next bit. "I won't be needing the poem."

Juliet opened her mouth, but no words emerged, only stunned disbelief. Finally, she recovered herself and pushed off the outcropping. "What do you mean you won't be needing the bloody poem?"

She stuck a hand down the front of her dress and began rummaging about, finally emerging with a neatly folded bunch of papers. She held them up accusingly. "I lost an entire night's sleep finishing this."

Rory crossed the short distance separating them and took the proffered papers. With the gibbous moon directly overhead, he was able to give the pages a quick scan. Five total, front and back, the script dense. "It's quite, erm, prodigious."

Juliet sniffed and lifted her chin. "I found a lot to say."

"About Miss Dalhousie?" he asked, skeptical.

"Well, about waterfalls and such."

He held a page close and squinted, just making out a few lines. "And about Hamish?"

She gave a one-shouldered shrug. "I figured she must love Hamish. Who wouldn't?"

"Miss Dalhousie, methinks," he said. Oh, why wouldn't they stop talking about that blasted woman? She was beside the point, entirely. "I've never seen her take to an animal now that I think on it."

Juliet's observant eye narrowed upon him. "You lied to me."

There they were. Some of the words that needed airing.

"Lie is a very strong word," he said. "More false pretenses than outright lies, I would say."

She exhaled a long-suffering sigh. "You sound like Archie."

Rory snorted. She wasn't wrong.

"Deceived," she amended.

That was a worse word.

It was only the naked, unfiltered truth that would do.

And even then, he wasn't so sure… But he had to try.

"I wanted to spend time with you," he said. "And I wasn't sure how."

"You could've asked."

"Truly?" he asked, incredulous. "Juliet—and I say this as a man who appreciates this quality about you—you're not exactly the most approachable lass."

Her eyebrows looked as if they might lift clear off her forehead. "That excuses you lying to me?"

"Perhaps a little."

She gasped. If the sun had been shining, he would've detected twin patches of scarlet blazing across her cheeks, he was certain. "Again, you're sounding like one of my cousins."

"Which one?"

"Take your pick."

"I think it's still Archie."

"You're being incorrigible."

He shook his head and took a step forward, closing more of the distance between them. "I'm simply a man trying to figure out how to be in the same room—or fairy glen—with the woman who has come to occupy his every waking thought and more than a few sleeping ones, too."

"By making me your fool."

"You could never be that."

She set her gaze on the narrow valley below.

"I'm madly in love with you, Juliet."

Her head whipped around. "You *love* me?"

"Aye."

"*You* love *me?*"

"Erm, aye."

She exhaled a sharp breath through her nose. "You certainly have an odd way of showing it. I spent all last night writing a poem to the woman you love."

"No, you didn't."

"The dark circles beneath my eyes this morning could attest to it."

"But you didn't," he insisted. "Not unless you wrote it to yourself."

Her mouth snapped shut. She was thinking.

Which could be good.

Or very, very bad.

"I…I must go," she said, moving toward the sheep scramble, her feet picking up pace with every step. "I need time with my thoughts."

"I understand," he said to her back. Juliet was a thinker. It was a large part of what made her Juliet.

And he loved Juliet. But…

"Juliet?"

She met his gaze over her shoulder.

"Allow yourself to feel, too," he called out, his heart in every word. "What we have is more than what we've shared with our bodies." He let that sit in the air for a moment. "Tomorrow evening…I'll see you at the play?"

Though a storm raged in her eyes, she nodded before resuming her descent down the hill.

Clearly, she wished to walk alone. He could respect that, but still he followed at a distance. After he watched her disappear safely through the wide double doors of the assembly rooms, he cut left, choosing to forego the rest of an evening of making idle conversation with neighbors and dancing with winsome daughters.

He'd never been skilled at faking jollity, so it was better he took himself off for a night's ramble.

Besides, he had a poem to read by his favorite poetess, and perhaps Hamish needed a lullaby sung to him.

He'd, indeed, made a hash of matters with Juliet.

But now she knew he had.

And somehow that was better—though it was also worse.

He would see her tomorrow night.

It was the brittle twig upon which all his hopes hung.

Chapter Fifteen

Next evening

JULIET LEANED AGAINST the back wall of the receiving hall and gave the tambourine in her hand a gentle shake, just enough to give a sense of wind whispering through trees.

Ambience, that was her role for the night—since she'd confessed to Delilah that she hadn't memorized her lines for Celia. Delilah had let out a tiny cry of frustration and thrown her hands into the air before marching off to find the youngest Dalhousie boy, Juliet's double.

Juliet gave the audience a quick once-over. Mostly villagers, who made for boisterous theatergoers. This would be no quiet and respectful Shakespeare production. Mr. and Mrs. Dalhousie sat in the front row, watching with differing levels of interest. It was only the first scene and Mr. Dalhousie had already nodded off twice, much to the chagrin of his wife, who jabbed a sharp, pointed elbow into his ribs every tenth line or so.

In truth, the play had gotten off to a decent start. At ten years of age, the youngest Dalhousie lad made a more than passable Celia. Although Juliet did feel a slight bit of guilt that her confession that she didn't know the lines for Celia was less confession than outright lie.

Of course she knew all the lines. Her mind had been stewing in Shakespeare since Delilah could read. Juliet knew them all from love-crossed Romeo to perfidious Goneril to loyal Miranda.

And watching the stage now, Juliet knew the lie for the correct decision. Otherwise, she'd be presently treading the boards with Rory, and she wasn't yet ready for close proximity to the man.

She hadn't even looked at him directly yet.

Which wasn't to say the edge of her vision wasn't tracking his every movement.

Frustrating peripheral vision.

A figure brushed past Juliet, snapping her to. James Dalhousie—or Orlando, as he'd insisted on being called for the last three days so he could stay in character—was making straight for a younger brother. Stealthily, he approached the boy from behind and wrapped an arm around his neck. The smaller boy put up a fight, but wasn't much of a match for his older brother who immediately wrestled him to the ground.

Even so, the younger brother didn't seem all that surprised at his fate. "Ah, James, leave off," his complaint a rasped murmur.

"It's *Orlando*," said James through gritted teeth.

Alarmed, Juliet rushed over and pulled at James' chartreuse velvet doublet that retained a whiff of ancient attic must. "What are you on about?" she hissed, so as not to alert the audience.

The lad shot her an annoyed glare over his shoulder. "Getting ready for my scene with Kilmuir."

"Ah," said Juliet. He was taking the challenge of wrestling Rory quite seriously. Did he not understand the concept of acting? She released his jacket and retreated a step. "Well, then, carry on."

And good luck to the lad when the time came. While he did possess the fire, he yet lacked the size to take on Rory. She only hoped Rory went easy on him.

Of course, he would. He was Rory.

He wasn't the sort with a burning need to prove his manhood.

An irritatingly attractive quality.

Juliet resumed her place at the back wall and picked up the

wind chime, letting the hollow tubes knock lightly together. *Ambience.*

Her eye immediately caught on Rory as he strode across the stage, wearing a…*kilt.*

She swallowed, her mouth gone suddenly dry.

Oh, how well the garment suited him…and his thick, muscled thighs. Even his calves showed to particular advantage through woolen socks.

She couldn't have been the only lady to notice—or feel that the room had grown warm.

He threw out his arm at an awkward angle as he spoke his lines a little louder than necessary. He was an atrocious actor. It was objective fact. He had to know it, but it didn't seem to bother him as he always went along with whatever japes the Windermeres planned.

She supposed she found that quality irritatingly attractive, too.

"I'm madly in love with you, Juliet."

Oh, those words… The look in his eyes when he'd spoken them. *Sincere…determined…*

Those words didn't speak to the girl who'd harbored a secret infatuation.

They spoke to the woman she was now.

The woman who was damnably angry with that damn fool man.

An entire poem… He'd had her write an *entire poem* for another woman.

That fool man… those three words were the only ones her brain had been able to form this morning.

It was easier to hold on to her anger that way. Otherwise, different words would try to worm their way in—words that would want to come to *that fool man*'s defense.

And she wasn't ready for those words.

Not yet.

A throat cleared at her side. Juliet tore her gaze away from

Rory to find a familiar—and somewhat unwelcome—figure at her side.

"Miss Dalhousie," she said. Perhaps she wouldn't notice Juliet's lack of enthusiasm. "Aren't you meant to be sitting in the audience?"

"I only just arrived and didn't want to interrupt the performance," Miss Dalhousie whispered, though there was hardly a need. The audience was growing decidedly rowdier in its appreciation of the performance. "I'll take my seat at the intermission."

"That's very thoughtful of you," said Juliet.

Miss Dalhousie…never put a foot wrong.

Juliet's eyes might've rolled just a little and she found herself asking, "Don't you ever feel the need to break the rules, Miss Dalhousie?"

Juliet's mouth snapped shut. She didn't have any right to ask that question.

A little smile ticked up the side of Miss Dalhousie's mouth as she shed her travel pelisse. "Sometimes."

Another impertinent question was falling from Juliet's mouth, "Then why don't you?"

"I suppose I'm not like one of you Windermeres."

Juliet relented. "Well, I am one of the tamer Windermeres."

"I admire that about you."

"What is that?"

"Your ability to balance your naturally reasonable nature with the Windermere wild streak that runs through you."

Juliet blinked. It was usually her making these uncomfortable observations about others. She wasn't sure she enjoyed being on the receiving end.

"I know someone else who admires that in you," continued Miss Dalhousie.

"Oh?" asked Juliet, striking the wind chime with more force than necessary.

Miss Dalhousie jutted her chin toward the stage. It was obvious who she meant. "Kilmuir."

Juliet scoffed and shook her head dismissively, decidedly uncomfortable discussing Rory with Miss Dalhousie.

But Miss Dalhousie, it seemed, had something to say. "Do you know why I refused his proposal of marriage two years ago?"

Juliet met the other woman's gaze. She did have the loveliest brown eyes that one could fall into. "No."

She'd never understood it.

"Because he didn't look at me in that specific way."

"What way is that?"

"The way he was looking at you at supper a week ago."

Juliet's heart might've stopped in her chest. She couldn't be certain, because she'd gone numb all over. "And what way is *that*?" she somehow asked.

"Like he is a planet in orbit to your sun."

Now it was Juliet's lungs refusing to move. "In addition to all your other numerous talents, are you also a poet, Miss Dalhousie?"

The other woman shook her head, her smile broadening. "Hardly," she said. "I'm simply speaking the truth as I see it."

Juliet set her wind chime down and faced Miss Dalhousie fully. It occurred to her that she might owe the woman an apology for disliking her for no better reason than she'd been the recipient of Rory's attention years ago. In truth, she'd never gotten to know Miss Dalhousie—the woman she truly was behind all her perfection and accomplishments. That was a wrong that needed to be righted.

But it was Miss Dalhousie who spoke first. "I admire something else about you, Miss Windermere."

"*Juliet*," said Juliet, taking Miss Dalhousie's hand. "You must call me Juliet."

"Juliet, you must call me Davina."

"A lovely name," said Juliet. "It suits you."

"I admire that you've always known what you wanted."

"And what do I want?" She was genuinely interested in what

this woman saw.

"To be free to write," said Davina. "You Windermeres seize your freedoms. You don't ask for them politely."

"Oh, you can't do that, Davina." On this, the ground was firm beneath Juliet's feet. "You can't ask. Take now, apologize later."

Davina smiled ruefully. "For all my accomplishments, 'tis not a skill I've developed, I'm afraid."

Juliet squeezed her hand. "You can do anything, Davina. I'm convinced of it."

"Mine are simply accomplishments that anyone can be taught. They don't originate from true desire. That has never come to me."

True desire.

At that moment, on stage, Rory stumbled into view, laboring beneath an object attached to his back. Except it was no object, but rather James Dalhousie attempting to wrestle Rory to the ground.

Miss Dalhousie lifted a hand to her mouth and stifled a giggle. "I'd heard that James was taking his acting duties rather too far."

All the stage and audience went uncomfortably silent—save James' grunts of exertion—as everyone watched, mesmerized, the spectacle of a lad of seventeen years and eight stone attempting to bring down a man of thirty-two years and fifteen stone. It defied all logic and good sense, and yet, as she watched, Juliet felt certainty swell alongside the befuddlement inside her.

True desire.

That man allowing himself to be awkwardly wrestled to the stage boards by a lad half his age and size—risking showing everyone precisely what a Scotsman wore beneath his kilt—was her true desire personified.

"I'm madly in love with you, Juliet."

When he, at last, allowed James to pin him to the boards and lay in faux defeat as the lad released an unseemly roar of triumph, a realization walloped Juliet over the head.

Love was war.

And Rory, the nicest, most decent man she'd ever known, had been fighting all this time.

For her.

"You're not exactly the most approachable lass."

He wasn't wrong.

In truth, he'd done everything to win her—even if he did have her labor over a poem for another woman.

The time had arrived…

For her surrender.

And what a sweet defeat it would be, for it would win her heart's desire. Yet…

She must fight, too.

To be worthy of him.

What was that nonsense that she never intended to marry?

Of course she did.

She fully intended to marry Rory.

Urgency filled her. It was only when she started to take a step toward the stage that she noticed her hand still holding the wind chimes. "Davina," she began, handing over the instrument, "you must visit Delilah in London soon. She'll be happy to teach you how to break a few rules, and she'll be glad for your company after—" Her mouth snapped shut.

"*After?*" Davina prodded, a knowing smile in her fathomless eyes.

After I run off with that man presently being pinned to the ground by a youth half his age and size.

But she couldn't very well say that.

Besides, the twinkle in Davina's eye suggested she'd intuited as much.

Juliet cleared her throat. "After, erm, Easter." It was as good a time as any, and honestly her interest in the matter had altogether deserted her.

"Easter was only last month," Davina pointed out.

"Yes," said Juliet, "that would be lovely." She had one more thing to say. The most important thing. "True desire will come to you someday, Davina, and leave you no choice but to follow it. You'll know when you find it."

And with a sure step Juliet began making her way up the center aisle, toward the stage.

Toward the man she was madly, irrevocably in love with.

Toward the man who would be hers.

After all, it was Shakespeare who said all the world was a stage—in the very play that was presently being enacted on those boards.

And within the black-and-white lines of a play wasn't there universal truth that infused words with meaning?

What better place to speak her heart and ask for a future with the man who would be hers, if he would have her?

Chapter Sixteen

Ten minutes earlier

RORY POKED HIS head around the curtain and gave the audience a quick scan. It wasn't until he squinted that he found Juliet standing against the back wall in the farthest reaches of the receiving hall, holding a…

Was that a wind chime in her hand?

And who was that standing beside her?

His stomach lurched. He might've groaned, too.

Miss Dalhousie.

The former object of his affection conversing with the woman he was determined to spend the rest of his life with.

That might not result in a positive outcome for him.

A throat cleared behind him. He turned to find Ravensworth giving his tatty, old kilt an amused up-and-down. Rory wouldn't be living this night down for a good long while, the duke's single lifted eyebrow said.

"Rory," said Ravensworth.

"Sebastian," Rory returned.

The amusement faded from Ravensworth's eyes, replaced with a purposeful glint. Rory knew that look. His friend had something to say.

At last, he said it. "Are you planning to do right by her?"

Rory didn't need to ask who *her* was. He supposed it had become obvious. "If she lets me."

That was the truth.

Ravensworth snorted. "Windermeres."

Indeed, *Windermeres.*

Ravensworth grew deadly serious. "Convince her."

Rory nodded and took a step, determined to do exactly that. A staying hand wrapped around his upper arm. "You're not thinking of going to her, are you?" said Ravensworth.

That was exactly what Rory was thinking.

She had to know they were perfect for each other.

"Didn't you just say—"

"Best to wait for a Windermere to come to you," said Ravensworth, his eye on the stage.

Rory followed the line of his gaze. *Ah.* "Like you've been waiting for a certain Windermere?"

Ravensworth flashed him an irritated glance.

Delilah was certainly a glory both on and off the stage—the sort to be flame to Ravensworth's moth. The man had an insatiable appetite for art, beauty, and talent, particularly when combined in one female form. And for all her wildness, Lady Delilah Windermere was all those things.

It was none of Rory's concern, of course, but he wished Ravensworth the best of luck.

He would need it.

A voice sounded behind them. "What is it we're looking at?"

Rory and Ravensworth turned in unison to find Oliver Quincy. A moment later the man answered himself. "Ah, the beauteous Lady Delilah."

Ravensworth's jaw clenched. Rory couldn't help an amused snort.

"You know," continued Quincy, impervious to the tension building around him, as ever. "I'm beginning to think she won't be accepting my standing proposal of marriage."

Ravensworth pinned the man with an incredulous glare. "Wasn't that proposal made three years ago?"

"Precisely," said Quincy, rocking onto his toes, self-satisfied.

Rory supposed he would ask the question that couldn't remain unasked. *"Precisely* what?"

"After all that kerfuffle and scandal she caused at Eton, I would still have her."

A dumbfounded beat of time skated past.

Quincy wasn't finished yet. "It takes some ladies longer than others to know what's good for them."

Another beat of silence descended betwixt the three men as it occurred to two of them those might've been the first sensible words ever to emerge from Oliver Quincy's mouth—though perhaps not in the way he intended.

"Right," said Ravensworth. "I'll be joining our hosts in the audience." He directed a parting nod toward Rory and a lifted eyebrow at Quincy.

"Psst," Rory heard from the curtain on stage left. Delilah was waving wildly, beckoning him forward onto the stage, where James Dalhousie waited, a pugnacious set to his jaw and a mean glint in his eye.

The time had arrived for the wrestling scene.

Best to get on with it.

Rory strode forward, and the lad ran at him full tilt and immediately attached himself to his back. While the audience thought they were watching actors play their roles, Dalhousie clearly felt differently as his arms tightened around Rory's neck and squeezed.

Rory had expected something like this.

As he allowed Dalhousie to "wrestle" him—males of teen years could be oddly fragile beings, for all their emerging muscles—Rory kept half an eye fixed on Juliet. She and Miss Dalhousie continued their talk. Clearly, the two women had much to get off their chests.

Then from his one good eye that wasn't presently pinned to the stage boards, he watched Juliet do something unexpected. She handed Miss Dalhousie her wind chimes and took a step.

A step up the center aisle…

His heart kicked up into a sprint.

A step toward him.

"That'll be enough," he muttered up to Dalhousie.

"I don't sense your spirit has yet broken, Kilmuir," the lad said through gritted teeth.

"If you'll recall, we're currently *acting* in a play." Rory couldn't help noting the curious, disbelieving silence that had descended on the receiving hall as Dalhousie gave his all. "Ye'll not be breaking my spirit today, lad."

"I'll say when it's over."

Enough was enough.

Dalhousie glued to his back, Rory pushed to all fours, and then shook off the lad as easily as water flew off Clootie's back. The confounded spell that had descended on the room at the sight of James Dalhousie wrestling Lord Kilmuir to the ground lifted, and the actors on stage snapped to and remembered their role, which was to escort a vanquished Charles the Wrestler off the stage.

Except in this version of the play, Rory was going nowhere, for Juliet now stood at the front of the stage and was staring up at him. "What ho!" she cried out as she clambered up onto the boards.

What was Juliet about, anyway?

Delilah was clearly wondering the same as she stared at her cousin, mouth agape, a storm building on her face, even as she tried to stay in character. "Who is this that has wandered into our fair woods?"

Juliet swiveled and proclaimed, "I am called Juliet."

It struck Rory that though Juliet excelled in the creation of words, that same level of talent didn't extend to her acting skills.

In short, she was a terrible actress.

Delilah looked tempted to drag her cousin off the stage. "I believe you've wandered in from an entirely different play, *Juliet*."

"Oh?" Juliet put her hand to her forehead and dramatically scanned the stage and audience. "O Macbeth, Macbeth, wherefore art thou Macbeth?" she proclaimed.

Delilah groaned. The other actors looked confused. Out in the audience, Mr. and Mrs. Dalhousie looked bewildered. Miss Dalhousie looked to be stifling a giggle behind her hand. Ravensworth leaned back in his chair and crossed his legs, as if settling in for a night's entertainment.

And Rory… Well, he found himself taking a step forward, a feeling of protectiveness surging within him. If Juliet was here to make a fool of herself, then she wouldn't be alone.

She would never be alone.

"'Tis your Macbeth, fair Juliet," he said.

Delilah threw frustrated hands into the air and lowered herself to a seat, legs crossed in front of her. She leaned back onto her elbows and watched, clearly resigned to the fact that she'd lost all control. The moment no longer belonged to the actors reciting lines, but to him and Juliet—playing none other than themselves, speaking the words writ upon their hearts.

Juliet stared out at him, vulnerable in a way he'd never seen before. What she was doing right now, being the center of attention, couldn't have been comfortable for her. But then, he was finding the course of true love wasn't exactly a comfortable business.

Or something like that.

Shakespeare said it better.

She rubbed her lips together, then opened her mouth. Then closed it. Then opened it again, decided. "The essence of something is the most difficult thing to describe, because the essence is the truth that lay at its very core—at its heart. Take love, for instance. It isn't a tangible object that can be held in a hand, and yet it can be held in a heart. It contains substance and solidity"—she pressed her palm to her chest—"*here*." She inhaled deeply, as if bracing herself. "I love you, my Rory. Not the *you* I beheld with girlish eyes, but the *you* I've experienced with my woman's heart—and body."

The audience's scandalized gasp sailed up to the rafters.

Rory didn't hesitate.

He reached for her hand and led them to the front edge of the stage. He hopped the short foot to the floor and turned, holding her tight as she descended. All eyes following them, rapt, he led her down the center aisle and to the front door, which Rivers had already opened, ever the butler to anticipate the needs of Dalhousie Manor's guests.

In silence, Rory led Juliet down the wide, stone staircase and across the gravel drive before stepping onto the green lawn that led toward the ha-ha. He'd formed an idea about speaking his heart beneath the stars, but this was Scotland in spring, and no two consecutive nights would have stars. Instead, the sky hung low with a thick blanket of clouds heavy with unfallen rain.

Still, he kept walking until they were beyond view of the house. The windows would surely have eyes.

Only then, with the song of night sung by crickets and warblers for company, Rory pulled Juliet to a stop. Inches separated them as they stood facing one another. He opened his mouth to speak first, and shut it. He'd said so much last night—all that was within his heart, in fact.

Tonight was Juliet's turn.

Her eyes bright with all that yet lay unspoken, she said, "I thought about writing you a poem."

"I would be honored."

He'd thought it was only the female sex who experienced skipped beats of the heart. But he'd just been proven wrong.

"But I didn't."

"Oh."

"Because my mind would take over and try to perfect what's in my heart if I commit it to pen and paper. And I don't want that. What is *here*"—she pressed her palm to her chest—"and *here*"— she pressed her other palm to his chest—"isn't in need of perfecting, for it's the poetry writ upon my heart by yours."

He nodded.

"I tend to think about matters too much," she continued.

"I'm always searching for the perfect words. But with you, Rory, none of that is necessary. With you, I'm allowed simply to *feel*—in my body and in my heart. My mind has naught to do with you and me. With you, I can simply *be*." Uncertainty entered her eyes. "But in truth, I don't understand what benefit *you* get out of the bargain."

Though they weren't standing in a grove of olive trees in the sun-drenched Tuscan countryside, but rather in a sodden stand of oaks, Rory spoke the words he should've said two years ago. "You look like someone."

Juliet's eyebrows drew together. "And who is that?" she asked, wary.

"Like the woman I'm supposed to spend the rest of my life with."

"Oh, Rory."

"You, Miss Windermere, are beautiful and intelligent and talented and wickedly funny—and wicked other places, too. You listen to me. You take me seriously. Many don't."

"They should," she said, near ferocious.

"See? *There.*"

"What?"

He chuckled and tucked his thumb beneath her chin, tipping her head back. "You have a bit of the she-wolf about you. That bodes well."

"For what?"

"Life in the Scottish Highlands."

He had yet more to say—and a question to ask.

"I love you, my bonny lass." His hand slid around to cradle the nape of her neck, drawing her toward him. "Will you consent to be my bride and spend all the rest of your days with me?"

"Yes," she whispered, her eyes watery with unshed tears.

"How do you feel about a small wedding?"

"Of two?"

"Three," he said. "We'll need the smithy."

"Perfect," she said, the Windermere daring streak running

through her emerald eyes, and then she surrendered to his kiss.
Life would never be boring with his wild Windermere bride.
And Rory wouldn't have it any other way.

Epilogue

One month later

MAIDEN OF WIND *and sky…*

The line resonated through Juliet as she stepped onto the pile of rubble that had once been part of Dun Sgathaich, the castle that had been built upon the ruins of Dun Scaith—Scáthach's mythical Castle of Shadows—and stared out across Loch Eishort toward the far-off hills of the Cuillins.

This was the air Scáthach had breathed.

Warrior til the day ye died…

Juliet didn't bother jotting the lines down. They were middling at best.

Movement below caught her eye. Rory was climbing up to the opposite set of ruins. Once, a drawbridge had connected the outcropping where the main castle sat with the mainland. Now, the drawbridge was deteriorated and gone, and the castle could only be accessed by scaling the thirty-foot cliff. As there wouldn't have been a drawbridge in Scáthach's time, Juliet imagined this was a closer experience to the Dun Scaith of yore, where young warriors had to prove their mettle by breaching the fortress.

Still, Juliet found herself calling out, "Be careful."

Rory tossed her a smile over his shoulder and kept climbing.

How like a wife she sounded.

A wife.

A gust of wind from the north whipped through her hair,

setting long tendrils free from the loose braid. No signs of civilization for miles around, this was the wildest place she'd ever experienced—a place carved down to its rawest elements. *Fight. Survive. Live. Die.*

The stakes ran high in a place like this, and it took a special kind of person to thrive here. Juliet didn't think she had it in her, but the man currently scaling a thirty-foot cliffside—*her husband,* impossibly—he did. Physically, he was built for it. But that was only exterior strength. It didn't mean much. Toughness of the mind, that was what it took, and what Rory possessed. Though only she saw it…and his tenants. They saw it, too. It was obvious in the respect they showed the laird of the manor who they considered mostly English—which was all down to Rory and the grit he hid behind those lopsided smiles of his.

Oh, how she adored this man.

Warrior of earth and Skye…

That was the line.

She grabbed the journal out of her knapsack and scribbled it down. Once finished, she noticed the folded paper peeking above the front cover.

Delilah's letter.

Juliet didn't need to open and read it again, for she'd memorized its contents.

This last month she'd shed so many tears of happiness. When she and Rory had announced their intention to marry, immediately… Over the anvil as she'd spoken her vows… On her wedding night in Rory's arms. The ever cool and composed Juliet Windermere—now Lady Kilmuir—had become a leaky bucket.

But the tears that sprang to her eyes now held happiness tinged with a note of sadness. In the gain of Rory—the love of her life…the center of her future happiness—there had been loss, too. It wasn't that she'd lost Delilah, or the bond only they shared, but never again would they be two halves of a whole.

Rory was her other half.

And someday, Delilah would find her other half, too—if she

would but see him.

Which was for Delilah to decide. Nay, not decide. 'Twas not a decision made with the head, but with the heart—not with reason, but *feeling*.

One large, masculine hand, then another, appeared on the cliff's edge near where Juliet sat, followed by Rory's head and shoulders, the muscles of his bare forearms tensing and releasing as he pushed himself up. She would never tire of seeing her husband exert himself physically.

A trace of desire rippled through her. She couldn't have predicted she'd be a lusty sort of wife, but here she was plainly lusting after her husband.

Cheeks bright and a bead of perspiration rolling down his cheek, he lowered to a seat beside her, shoulder to shoulder, and reached for her hand, twining his fingers through hers. He jutted his chin toward Delilah's letter. "We'll see her when we're in London in August," he said, intuiting the direction of her thoughts.

"Actually," said Juliet, "I don't think we shall."

Rory's eyebrows lifted. "Oh?"

"She mentioned in the letter that she would be visiting a friend in Switzerland through the summer. We shouldn't expect her back until October."

"Which friend?" asked Rory, idly, as he pulled a pasty from the knapsack.

"Indeed," was Juliet's reply. Delilah hadn't said, and Juliet knew that meant one thing. *Trouble.*

"She's hatched a plan, hasn't she?" Rory asked around a bite of pasty.

Leave it to Rory to cut to the quick of the matter. She loved that about her husband.

"She has," said Juliet.

You set your gaze upon the world…

The line didn't scan with the other, but she liked it. She wrote it down.

"Here." Rory held out his half-eaten pasty. "You must try this."

Juliet already knew there was no point in resisting. "You're constantly feeding me, husband."

His turquoise gaze turned serious. "You need to be ready."

"And what is it I need to be ready for?"

He glanced down at her stomach, and she reflexively rubbed her hand across its still-flat expanse. Her menses were nearly two weeks late, but she hadn't yet mentioned it to Rory as she didn't want to spark hope. But now…with a bright summer sun shining on them and the air scented with gorse and sea…perhaps now was, in fact, the perfect time to speak it aloud. "Rory, the possibility may exist that I'm—" A knot of emotion formed in her throat. Here they were again. Those blasted tears.

Rory reached a strong arm around her shoulders and pulled her close. "Aye, lass."

He'd noticed.

Of course he had.

His hand covered hers on her stomach, and they stared together out across the loch toward the brown and gold Cuillins. "What a place Scáthach built for herself," said Juliet, and other words flowed, too, as she wrote them down. *Upon you they gazed and found not fearsome hero but undeserving girl.*

This line didn't scan either, but it would get there. For all its frilly reputation, the composition of poetry was hard toil and certainly not for the faint of heart.

A moment beat by before Rory said, "My warrior poet."

"I'm not sure Scáthach would've found use for a warrior poet. I suspect she'd have much preferred an ability to wield sword over quill."

Rory directed his lopsided smile at Juliet. As ever, a melting sensation spread from dark, deep-set parts of her that only his smile touched.

"Ah," came a velvet rumble from the depths of his chest, "but that would've been her loss, and certainly my gain."

He tugged her closer, and his head angled so he caught her mouth with his.

As sparks flew through her and lit into flame that only her husband could slake, a thought came to her.

No longer did she wish this man to take a flying leap off Ben Nevis.

And if he ever did, she would be right there, taking flight alongside him.

The End

About the Author

Sofie Darling is an award-winning author of historical romance. The third book in her Shadows and Silk series, Her Midnight Sin, won the 2020 RONE award for Best Historical Regency.

She spent much of her twenties raising two boys and reading every romance she could get her hands on. Once she realized she simply had to write the books she loved, she finished her English degree and embarked on her writing career. Mr. Darling and the boys gave her their wholehearted blessing.

When she's not writing heroes who make her swoon, she runs a marathon in a different state every year, visits crumbling medieval castles whenever she gets a chance, and enjoys a slightly codependent relationship with her beagle, Bosco.